WITHDRAWN
UTSA LIBRARIES

Getting to Know the Weather

A list of books in the series appears at the end of this volume.

GETTING TO KNOW THE WEATHER

Stories by

Pamela Painter

UNIVERSITY OF ILLINOIS PRESS

Urbana and Chicago

*Publication of this work was supported in part
by grants from the National Endowment for the Arts
and the Illinois Arts Council, a state agency.*

©1985 by Pamela Painter
Manufactured in the United States of America
C   5   4   3   2   1

This book is printed on acid-free paper.

"The Next Time I Meet Buddy Rich," *North American Review,* 1979
"Intruders of Sleepless Nights," *Ploughshares,* 1982. Reprinted in *The
    Ploughshares Reader: New Fiction for the Eighties,* 1985
"The Visitor," *Literary Review,* 1983
"Night Walk," *Florida Quarterly,* 1976
"The Sorting Out," *Transatlantic Quarterly,* 1974
"Something to Do," *Open Places,* 1985
"Sylvia," *Ascent,* 1976. Reprinted in *The Things That Divide Us,* 1985
"Patterns," *Descant,* 1975
"A Man of His Time," *Chicago Magazine,* 1979
"Winter Evenings: Spring Night," *Epoch,* 1974
"Suppertime," *Literary Review,* 1977
"The Kidnappers," *North American Review,* 1984
"Getting to Know the Weather," *Sewanee Review,* 1985

Library of Congress Cataloging in Publication Data

Painter, Pamela.
    Getting to know the weather.

    (Illinois short fiction)
    I. Title.
PS3566.A36G4   1985   813'.54   84-24148
ISBN 0-252-01195-3 (alk. paper)

LIBRARY
The University of Texas
At San Antonio

For Robie

Contents

The Next Time I Meet Buddy Rich

We pulled into town just as the sun was coming up, dropped some stuff off at the rooms they gave us, and took the drums and other instruments over to the club. The debris of empty glasses, full ashtrays, disarranged chairs was still there from the night before, heavy with stale air. I unrolled my rug, set up my drums. Felt for the piece of gum Buddy Rich once gave me—now stuck at the bottom of the floor tom-tom. Vince hooked up the sound system and then we headed back to the hotel.

I carried in my practice set, calling to Gretel to open the door. Finally I used my key. Sounds of the shower running droned from the bathroom. Her clothes were scattered over a chair, suitcases sprawled open on the floor. Then the water went off and Gretel appeared in the doorway with a towel around her, a folded rim keeping it in place, flattening her breasts. Her hair was piled on her head and held by one barrette. Beads of moisture gleamed on her shoulders, her legs.

"No more hot water," she said, as she pulled the barrette from her hair, shaking it loose. "I'm getting tired of these places. This is too far away from the club considering we're going to be here two weeks."

"We can move. We have before."

"It's the whole scene," she said pointing to the suitcases. "Where's it going? I know what you want. But sometimes wanting isn't enough."

I lay down on the bed and closed my eyes. I saw her standing in the towel. I took the towel away and looked at her full breasts, her stomach, a different texture of hair.

"Sorry," she said. "You want to listen now or later?"

"Later." I put the towel back and opened my eyes. She was looking out the window. I felt sorry for her living this way, but the words to change it all, to take me back to Erie, just wouldn't come. "Let's have a nice dinner after the club run tonight. Chicago doesn't close down like Kansas." She shrugged her shoulders. She was right. If you weren't playing, it was hard to care what you did out here. One room after another. A hundred tables in a hundred towns. The bed slid as I got up. I licked some of the water off her right shoulder. She didn't move.

"OK, later," she said. And I understood that everything would have to wait. That was OK too. She had been traveling with me for the past year, ever since we decided we'd eventually get married. We never mentioned settling down, but I could tell she was tired of being on the road. The band probably wouldn't be together much longer anyway with Jack pulling toward hard rock. Then I'd take my uncle up on his offer of being a plumber for him again. *That* I didn't want to think about.

So I arranged my practice set, fitting it around my chair. Settling it into the sparse pile of the rug to make it steady. "Bring me back two ham on rye," I told Gretel when Jack and Vince knocked on the door.

Vince understood. Five years I've been breaking my ass to get the big break, trying to make it happen. One night in Columbus I was talking to a drummer who was almost there, would be in a few years — by thirty you have to be. That's what I asked him. "How do you get there?"

He wiped his hands under his arms and said, "You practice your ass off all your life and the better you get the worse you seem to yourself and you're ready to give up; and then one day when your hands aren't getting any faster you say the hell with it. When you next sit down at a set of drums after you haven't touched them for days, weeks, like a vow you'd made — suddenly you're doing all the things you've been trying to do for years — suddenly there is a 'before' and 'after' and it's the 'after' where you are now — and goddamn you don't know why, you just know that you're finally there. Then it's only a matter of time."

And now my time was running out. The band close to breaking up. Kids, pets, hard rock up against the slower stuff. I looked down at my hands. Clean, now. The prints clean, sensitive to the smooth surface of the sticks. I hated being a plumber although I was good at it. All that grease, fitting pipes, welding. I straightened my back. Time enough for planning that later. Time to practice now. I pulled back the plastic curtains to let in the last of the hotel's sun. Then I started to play. Slow at first, just letting my wrists do the work, looking out past the sunken single beds, past the cheap print of some flower, using a little pressure, feeling how my wrists were somehow connected with the tension in my feet. Just feeling it happen like I was watching myself in the mirror. Trying for the sounds of Buddy Rich.

The next time I meet Buddy Rich it'll be at a 76 station in some crazy place, like Boone, Iowa, not at a concert, and he'll be all burnt out waiting for a cup of coffee and I'll go up to him and say—what I'll say I haven't worked out yet but it'll happen and I'll say it then.

I met Buddy Rich for the first time at Rainbow Gardens in Erie, Pennsylvania. I was playing a spot called The Embers and it was our night off. We went really early, to get good seats up close so I could watch him play, watch his hands and feet and the way his body moves. He's a karate expert—once said that the martial arts apply to drumming; they key your mind up for getting into it, coordinate your hands and feet. I want to ask him about this when I meet him next.

The Rainbow Gardens is an oval-shaped arena, a stage at one end and a big wooden dance floor in the middle of a bunch of tables. Loads of people and glasses and cheap booze. It was during intermission, on my way back from the john, that I saw him. He was sitting off to the side, just happened to be there—probably after changing his shirt. Not drinking, just leaning back in his chair. Looking out as if to say, "OK, show me something intelligent."

I walked past thinking, "That can't be." Somehow you think of stars as either living on stage or in their dressing rooms. No real life, no tired hands. Then I walked past again and got enough nerve to say, "Buddy Rich?" and he didn't say "no," so I went on and said,

"I'm Tony — I'm a drummer and I play with Circuit of Sound." The words kind of rushed at him like a spilled drink and just as effective. "I think your band is really great," I said. He seemed to lean further back in his chair. He had on a long-sleeved grey shirt and grey pants. His fingers were tapping on the table, tapping like they were just doing it by themselves. I fumbled in my wallet for a card with the name of my band on it. "Would you autograph this for me," I said. I gave him a pen.

His first words were, "Who do you want it to?"

"Tony," I said, "and good luck on the drums."

He looked at me kind of funny and then wrote, "Best Wishes." I nodded, disappointed. Then I thanked him and went back to my seat, knowing I had blown my chance. Where are the questions when it matters? I wished I could grab him by the collar and say, "Hey, I'm different. I'm not like all the rest of the people who don't understand what Buddy Rich is unless you're in solo. Who don't understand that you, Buddy Rich, are here for the band — while all these people are here for Buddy Rich." But I didn't say it. I drank down eight ounces of Schlitz — chugging it to drown my embarrassment, and dying a second time because I finally realized that he thought I meant good luck to him on the drums. As if he needed it. Shit.

I let about ten minutes pass. Watching him just sitting there, wanting to know what was going through his mind, wanting to know what was keeping his hands moving or still. What's in his mind when he's playing. He had a back operation in July and a night later he was on the bandstand, behind the drums. Later, on a talk show he said they should have done the operation while he was playing, then they wouldn't have needed an anesthetic.

Finally, I couldn't stand it anymore. I chugged another Schlitz and stood up. I hadn't talked to my date since I sat down and all I could do now was tap her under the chin — grateful that she understood.

"I talked to you a few minutes ago and nothing came out right — including asking for your autograph," I said. He seemed to appreciate my honesty because his eyes stayed on me longer and again I told him how great he and his band were and he said, "sit down," so I pulled out a chair across the table from him. Then I started to pinpoint all the different songs that I really enjoyed off his albums — some of them almost unknown. I counted on that. Like "Goodbye Yesterday," like how it talks to me instead of playing.

"It shows how close the musicians work — you know the music is in front of them, but no arranger, no charts could do it for you — it's the energy of the group that pulls it together, that makes it talk." I told him this and more about "Preach and Teach," and he was nodding his head and not leaning back anymore. Now he leaned forward on his table, looking at me. "You know," I said, "with you, it's not just jamming. It's structure pushed to the end in sound." We sat in silence for a few minutes thinking about it.

"Yeah, you do understand," he said. Then he kind of grinned that wide smile of his. "Hard to talk about, isn't it. Easier to play."

"If you're you," I said. "I'm still trying."

"You know," he said, "interviewers are always asking me about the future of music. Hell I don't know about that. For me it's playing two hours here then going down the road to Muncie, Indiana. It's the next night for me. Nothing more." His hands were still now and I saw them for the first time.

"You don't have any calluses," I said.

"Hell no I don't." He grinned again, spreading his fingers on the table. "If the pressure's right the sticks don't rub." Smooth. Magic.

Just then I noticed some kids standing off to the left of us waiting with their pencils and papers — finally having figured out who he was and who I wasn't. So I stood up to give them their turn and he reached out and grabbed my wrist. "Don't go," he said, "I'm not done talking to you." So I sat down. My wrist was burning and I knew that the next time I played, the next time my right hand had to make itself heard, it wouldn't be the same. "Sit down," he said, "I got a few more minutes before I have to play to this airport hangar." He gestured around the arena, the high steel-beamed ceiling, the cold aluminum walls painted yellow, pink, blue. It would never be the same for me again.

He held out his hand for pencils and paper and a guy stepped forward, a couple more shuffling behind him. Wondering who I was, sitting there like a friend.

"I really like your 'Sing, Sing, Sing,'" he said to Rich. Rich looked up at me sideways and winked and told him, "I'm going to play 'SSS' and 'Wipeout' in a medley just for you." The dumb ass should have known it was Krupa's theme song. I suddenly had a feeling for what Buddy Rich had to deal with, wanting to be liked and understood and yet running into people who kill off any generosity you feel for the public out there. Like the ones who come to hear his band — they're all looking for the drum solo — you can see their eyes light up as if the stage lights suddenly got switched around. They don't understand the dynamics and togetherness. They know the finished product in a half-assed way, but not how it comes about. Even the critics in the early days would say he plays too loud, or throws rim shots in where they don't belong. *Now* they know what they're hearing.

We talked for a few more minutes — then he said he had to go. Gave me a stick of gum — Dentyne. He stood up and leaned over the table and did a quiet roll with his hands to my shoulder. "I think you'll make it," he said. "I'll be hearing you some day." And he was gone. I guess I heard the rest of the concert. But now being there meant something else to me. And when I hit home that night the stick of gum went into my drum. Was there now. A small pink lump. I look at it just before I begin to play.

Gretel still wasn't back so I practiced a while longer. Then I moved to the bed and lay back, still hearing the sounds, my own sounds this time, and I lay there for one hour. Not sleeping but waiting for show time to come round. When she arrived with the sandwiches I ate them. When Vince called to check the program I talked. But I was hearing other things, I was making my own program for tonight.

Finally, I must have slept for a few hours because pretty soon Vince was pounding on the door yelling, "how we going to make it without our practice?" I knew what he meant. He plays a cool sax — sliding notes around like melted butter then pulling them together with a tension that tells in his back, in the way his arms move toward his sides when he gets up for his solo run. We might have made it, Vince and I; maybe he'll keep something together. "Meet you in the lobby," I yelled.

We took three changes of costume and all went in one van over to the club. We were starting out tonight in tuxes, then switching to sequined jump suits that remind me of kids' Dr. Denton pajamas, ending up in jeans. All a part of the act. Jack was driving and putting on his cuff links at the same time. He's a good guitarist and up-front man. Can talk to anyone—sifting his smile out over the audience behind his velvety voice. Carol, the vocalist, and he were a good pair. She was filing her nails. Gretel was out shopping.

The stage loomed in the back of the place away from the bar and the lighting was OK. Bad was bad. OK was good. There were a few early drunks sitting around before going home to the wife and kids and mashed potatoes—they'd be moving along as soon as the sound built—it always happened. I took a run on my drums—did some rolls —soft then faster and faster. I hit each drum firm, getting that crisp beat, starting with the snare and ending up with the floor tom-tom and then one closing beat on the bass to cut it off sharp. I set out two sets of new sticks because I've been breaking one or two a night. Then I rolled up my pant legs and sat there sipping coffee. Vince was off talking to the waitresses, trying to line something up for later— much later. It's hard—you have fifteen minutes here and there to make contact, change clothes, and sound like you're not coming on too strong. He's good-looking in a seedy sort of way and even then he's about 90 per cent unsuccessful. I just let it happen if it's going to. Sometimes classy groupies show up two, three nights in a row and you know they want to be asked out. Sometimes they think you'll be a temporary drug source, but they got us all wrong. If we find it we use it, but we don't travel with the stuff. Or play. If cops are even a little suspicious in some of those one-horse towns they'll rip your van apart in the middle of a cornfield—drum sets, suitcases, instruments, speakers, music. It happened once when Jack had some coke from another musician at a gig. But it wasn't on us. Who the hell wanted to be looking for bail in Boone, Iowa.

We were about ready to play, so I changed into my high-heeled shoes for a better angle. We started out with show songs, dance music —moving toward two shows a night. My solo is in the second. I usually start light, play something basic that people can tap their feet to. Then I build up by getting louder, and faster, bringing it back down to nothing then building to a finale with a very fast single-stroke roll. My sticks are moving so fast you can't see them. People relate to a set of drums before any other instrument—I guess because it's obvious what a drummer does—it's so physical.

We started playing and people began coming in. The usual crowd
—single people needing movement and noise, countermen, clerks
from the local record and sheet-music stores. Bored couples. And a
drummer or two. I've met one or two in at least half the towns. Some
I looked forward to seeing, some I hated running into again.

We didn't get any requests yet. That'd come later in the evening
after a show, after Carol went into her act. A few songs. Talking at
the tables, telling women about the men they're with, always on their
side. Gretel wasn't here yet. I missed her. But it wasn't reason enough
to make her want to stay.

While we were playing "Preach and Teach" something felt different. I moved into a double stroke roll. Not too loud, just testing. It
was a feeling. And then I was going faster and my sticks were almost
floating across the drums, washing the high hat, the cymbal and
snare with rushes of sound. Solid sound. And suddenly I knew I had
to stop right there. It was happening and I wasn't going to let it happen yet. Gretel still wasn't here. And I was afraid of what it meant for
both of us. But I had to be sure so I changed into a quiet single
stroke, hearing the sounds I've heard on my Buddy Rich albums, and
my hands were going places they hadn't been before, moving to beats
I'd dreamed of playing, sounds I'd played in my sleep, and tonight
they were mine. They were in my muscles and fingers as if they'd always been there—even though I knew they hadn't, but this time I
hoped they weren't ever going away.

I slowed way down as Jack went into his bass solo and then we
took one more run at the chorus before ending. Then I sat there feeling the sticks in my hands, rolling them between my fingers like
magic wands. I felt my back relax and curve into a tighter arc as I sat
there marking that place and that time. The bar stretching off into
the distance of lights and neon noise. Gretel now at our table center
front. Gretel in her beaded Indian blouse. My brown coffee mug on
the floor beside a bottle of Schlitz. Me at the drums, at twenty-six.

We took a break and I changed into my jump suit fast. Then I
joined Gretel at the table. I wanted to tell her but first I wanted her to
hear it—without words getting in the way. Anyway she avoided my
eyes so I ordered a beer. The tables were filling up. Sounds, smells

starting to multiply into that magic of late-night movement. A girl at the next table raised her glass to me. She had beautifully manicured nails — painted green. I nodded politely. "I went to the bus station today. Checked out the fare to home," Gretel said, finally looking at me. Her eyes were tired. She used to look more alive slaving in the Head Start program where she was working when we met. "But I didn't get the ticket yet."

"Is that what you want?" I asked. My stomach felt like a drum tuned too tight. I knew what she wanted but now I wasn't sure I'd ever get the whole thing together. I covered her hand with mine.

"I don't know what I want anymore," she said. "This just isn't enough even if we wanted the same thing. You big and famous on the drums. Us." She looked around the noisy room and I followed her glance to the stage, to the light glinting on the steel rims of the drums.

"We *are* us," I said but she didn't hear.

"I mean what makes someone give up. I feel like giving up and you're still out there playing." There were tears in her eyes and she blinked fast to spread them away.

"You want to know where being on the road ends for us?" I asked. She pulled her hand away, but I caught her fingers, could feel the turquoise ring I'd given her. "You're afraid I won't know." I knew she was because I had the same fear — living on a dream till the real end of everything. It was almost enough to walk me out of that club, my arm around her, the sticks and drums left behind. Almost enough.

She nodded. "And I know I'd keep asking. Wanting two things at once. Like I don't want to go now but I think I'm going anyway. For a while. Maybe I'll be back in a week. Round trip." She wiped her eyes and laughed up at me. It was a laugh too weakly struck to carry, but, God, I loved her for that smile. Then she clinked her glass with mine.

"I might get home before you do," I said. I missed her already. Her waiting for me at tables. Sleeping, turning when I turned. Her trivia games on the road as we zigzag across Route 80 just to break the monotony, getting off to the county roads for a while.

"Don't say that, Tony. I don't want to expect you."

She was right. There was nothing for me to say that I could say.

Vince and Jack were back on stage, tuning up. The others were coming back fast. I gave her hand a squeeze. "I have to play. We'll talk later."

"I'll be back for the last show," she said. The light played on the beads of her blouse as she sighed. Softer than drums. Her lips smiled. I kissed her fast. I loved her, but I left to play.

Close to the next break I looked out through the haze, the smoke now thick with words, perfume sprayed on too heavily in the ladies' room. Through the conversations, words going as much past the other person as our music, past people not used to listening to anything beyond their own pulse. And with the drums I had two. I looked out through this, looked for the few who made it all come together, for the one person alone, here for listening. The one who was watching my hands go to where they're supposed to be, craning his neck to watch my feet make the beat.

These people were the ones I leaned toward, the ones I played to. They knew it, and I knew they knew it. And sometimes during a break I would go and sit at their tables. I listened to things Buddy Rich must have heard a million times. But I'm not tired of it yet, maybe because it wasn't true—that I'm the greatest. But I liked to hear it and I talked back, I looked at them straight. It was the same way I played. Sometimes they couldn't handle it—me coming to them, my hand on the back of a chair ready to join them if asked— maybe they didn't have the next three questions memorized—so I moved on. I loved them just the same, but I moved on, doing us both a favor. A time and a place and all that crap. I've been there.

That night I sat with Harry Ratch, an ex-drummer turned history teacher. He told me that once in St. Louis he sat in three nights for Flip Belotti when he had an emergency operation. Harry was the high school hero. History went down pretty easily for the next few months.

I ordered a beer, keeping my limit of two while playing. Harry Ratch was drinking beer too. He was past the physical fitness of a drummer—it was hard to be overweight in this business—but I could tell by the way his arms moved, his shoulders moved, that he once sat behind a set. Suddenly I saw myself ten years from now sitting in The Embers in Erie, Pennsylvania. Talking to some young kid. Telling him about the time I talked to Buddy Rich. Pulling my back straight to hide the tire around my waist. Hoping he'll offer to let me take a turn at his drums. Wishing I hadn't had three drinks already.

It hadn't happened yet. I focused back on Harry Ratch. He told me that Flip Belotti said the thing for beginners is to always practice. "If you're right-handed, do it with your left. There's always practicing to be done when you're not behind the drums." Harry was passing this advice along to me. I accepted it graciously. It made sense. I told him I hoped to see him again in the next two weeks. Maybe he could sit in on a couple of numbers. For a moment his eyes lost their sad history.

"I'll be here," he said sitting back. "I'll be here." It felt good to make someone's night.

I broke my sticks in one of the first numbers and started working with a new pair. Then we began to play the medley that led into my solo. Again I just moved into the drums. I held off till the last moment, catching the beat at the last possible second, almost afraid to know if it stayed, afraid to trust my knowing. But man it was there.

I could feel it again and I listened to my wrists making music I was born to hear. I was loose and tight at the same time. My wrists were loose and my forearms were keeping the pressure under control. I was arching over the set. I looked for Gretel and she was watching. And she knew. I was playing the answer. Her eyes were sad and happy at the same time; her hands flat on the table, still. And I was moving back and forth toward the sounds I needed to make, toward the sound Vince heard because he stood up, and — still playing — he turned and saluted me with his sax. I knew he was hearing what was happening to me as my legs were tight against my jeans and my feet were wearing shoes I didn't feel and I thought: this is what I always wanted to know from Buddy Rich. What do you feel? When I'm as fast as you are, will I feel what you feel, will I know?

These questions went through my head like lightning, their smell remained, and now it was what I knew that stopped me thinking. That pulled my sounds out of the forest of tables and noise like an ancient drum in some tribal ritual. It was my night. I heard the voices in the club lose their timbre, saw heads turn. There was no going back to Erie, only nights like these to keep me whole.

People were standing now. And Harry Ratch must have felt in his heart that he was helping me to what he never made. I was glad he was here to help me move, and then there were no more voices. One by one the band was dropping back and out, and only Vince and I were left — his fluid notes winding around the sticks I was moving but no longer felt. We were making circuits of sound. He turned facing me, leaning into his sax, giving his pledge with the notes he made before he too dropped out and I was left. I was dripping wet and winging it. The spotlight hung before me like a suspended meteor. I played as if waiting for it to hit.

Intruders of Sleepless Nights

They own no dogs; the maid sleeps out. The catches on the windows are those old-fashioned brass ones, butterfly locks. No alarm system or fancy security. He memorized everything Nick had to tell about this job. He pulls on black cotton gloves, soft and close like ladies' gloves. He is no longer just a man out for a late-night walk as he enters this strange driveway wearing black gloves — if the cops come they would be hard to explain away. The porch is just like Nick described it, screened in, running the entire back length of the house. He mounts the brick steps slowly, slits the screen and opens the door. Listens. These small pauses set him apart from other second-story guys he knows, take time away from the seven minute in-and-out rule. But he ain't never been caught. He pulls a roll of masking tape and a straight-edged knife from his jacket pocket. Nick said the easiest window opens into a bathroom off the front hall. Two over from the back door. Quickly the taped asterisk takes shape — corner to corner, up and down. He always varies the pattern, uses different width tape. As he hits the window sharply, once, in the center, it splinters and holds. He folds the sagging shards of glass outward toward him, loosens more from the caulking, and puts them on a wicker table. Once more he listens — not taking Nick's word for everything. He hopes the sound wasn't loud enough to wake the sleeping couple eleven rooms and two floors away.

Her husband is asleep — finally. His back is to her, his right shoulder high, and now his breathing has slowed to a steady pace like some temporarily regulated clock. She has been lying on her back, staring at the ceiling, her silence a lullaby for him. Now she lifts her arms lightly from the bed, readjusting the blankets, placing more folds between them. She thinks of her husband as the mountain range to her lower plain in their nightly landscape. She flexes her fingers, her toes, stretches her legs until her tightness leaves, absorbed by the bed. She feels an energy at night that she cannot use by day, moving around this house with too many rooms. If she were alone — in some other, smaller place — she would live at night. Who else is up at this time while her husband dreams of secretaries and waitresses. Should she buy twin beds, electric blankets, or a divorce attorney? Or new garbage cans to foil those damn raccoons!

His wife thinks he is sleeping. He knows this by the way she begins to move, adjusting the sheets, almost gaily like a puppet released to life. He dislikes being able to fool her so easily, and sometimes he varies his breathing just to feel her freeze — he hopes, into an awkward unnatural position that hurts. But usually the game bores him, he'd rather sleep. He sleeps better with his girl friend, Nan, when they finally go to sleep after making love, after a last nightcap. "What an old-fashioned word," she said. Nan will be listening to PBS, propped up in bed with three or four books, cigarettes, ashtray, crackers, nail polish, cotton balls, a miniature magnetic chess set, a hair brush. Nan lives on crackers — wheat thins, water biscuits, matzo, almak. She likes to brush her hair as she watches television though it makes him nervous. He is ahead of her in games won at chess. Barely. He hears a noise somewhere near the library or patio. Raccoons again. They have both heard it, he can tell.

Carefully he removes the remaining shards of glass from the edge. Then he twists, first to put his head and arms through, then his shoulders. He can't see a thing. The room smells too sweet. His stomach heaves as he dives slow motion toward the sink. His belt pings softly against something, his hands find the sink's edge, the curve of the toilet seat. He balances unevenly for five seconds while he drags his legs across the windowsill. Finally he lowers himself to the floor which he has taken for granted. He sits on the soft carpet, breathing hard, and lets his eyes adjust to the light. Then he pulls a nylon stocking over his head, stretching it out near his eyes, pushing back his hair, raising and lowering his eyebrows. He stands to squint into the mirror at a face even his own mother couldn't finger. Next he locates the back door, leaving it open and ready for a fast exit.

What will Cola think if she buys twin beds, or say to friends, trains of cleaning women going home to Chicago's South Side. Friends who pass the talk on to "their women" as they call them. She herself hears a lot of gossip this way, making Cola a sandwich for lunch in their particular reversal of roles. Cola has five children to her own two, and a husband she gives a weekly allowance of $10.00 — to keep him coming round to see the kids. They both know, but don't say, what else for. She considers getting up to read, write letters to the children, an old roommate from college, or Betty Ford — "was the face-lift really necessary" — but she never does. She is more aware of herself at these times than any other. It might have something to do with the thin nightgown she wears, her breasts loose and flat. Sometimes she lies perfectly still and tries to feel the silk against her stomach, her thighs. She regrets that her mind's eye has no picture of herself naked as a young woman. She sees herself dusting, running the vacuum cleaner, shopping for a china pattern. She would like to do her own cleaning again.

For the hundredth time he wonders where he will go if he leaves. What will he take from this house as perfectly arranged as a stage set. He has not yet said "when" even to himself. Nan has given him a deadline but he knows he'll let it pass. He stopped counting deadlines — they and the bright cheerful women who make them after an elegant dinner or as he is about to turn off the bedside light are all gone. But the children are gone too, and that was the deadline he made himself when they were still in high school and he slept in spite of the Rolling Stones, or maybe because of. Then, the woman was Francine — he thinks? He doesn't know this woman next to him any more. She reminds him of the sad aging ladies who sell the perfume and lingerie he buys for Nan. She could be the owner of a smart mauve boutique, or an efficient travel agent, glasses dangling on a gold chain —

should he suggest this? Sometimes he is surprised to see her across from him at breakfast, as if the maitre d' has doubled up on tables. He is having more and more trouble sleeping next to her. What *does* she want? As in, "What do *those* women want?"

He locates the silver in the dining room to retrieve on his way out. He pulls open the usual shallow drawer and the forks and knives gleam dully like rows of fresh dead trout. Then he returns to the pantry, where the maid's stairway opens onto an upper landing which leads to the second floor, to the master bedroom where the woman keeps her jewelry. He has memorized the floor plan sketched by a nervous Nick over a couple of beers at Tandy's. The other guys left them alone when they moved to a booth, carrying their beers and Nick's first sketch on a napkin. You can always tell when someone is planning a job, the way they lean together, taking the beer slower than usual, and you know to leave them alone. No one says this, it just happens. But he and Nick can't go on much longer, been four years already—Nick, the inside man giving inspections on insurance riders, sitting in living rooms of the rich, taking notes about rings and things while drawing the floor plan in his head. Shit—forgetting to mark the uncarpeted stairs. He'll have to take it slow up the sides.

What will she do? She feels divorce coming like unreported bad weather, even though her husband has been giving her cheery predictions each of the past eight years she brought it up. Divorces have left two friends with large empty malevolent houses, looking for work in a young woman's world of Olay. Could she get thin again—she isn't fat but curves seem to have gone to the wrong places like misdirected traffic. She has stopped hoping for airline crashes, car accidents, a coronary as her husband straddles his most recent girl friend who, she knows, wears Chloe. It was the dream that did it—when they were selling the grand piano a year ago. Even now she shivers, sending ripples across the cover of the bed as she recalls that early morning dream before dawn. A man's voice, rough like some milkman or mailman's, said "I just killed your husband. You owe me ten thousand dollars." Finally she woke sweating and wet to the shrill sound of the phone across her husband's empty side of the bed. She answered the seventh ring, terrified, but hoping; it was some early riser who wanted to make sure the piano was his. Her disappointment turned petulant, she told him, "you're too late." She was shaking as she hung up the phone — alone, still married to a man probably very much alive. That squeak — like Cola on the stairs.

He resents her relaxed movements when she thinks he's asleep. He himself lies there tense, missing Nan, finally drifting into a dense exhausted sleep where he dreams of moving into his first apartment, an orange U-haul and four drinking friends to help. His wife — and Nan — are both waiting for him. The apartment has one bedroom but two kitchens, although neither woman cooks. He wakes with stomach cramps before he has to choose whose dinner he will eat. He practices saying, "I want a divorce." But he would have to turn to her. Even now, even thinking it, his back feels vulnerable. When he sleeps with Nan she curves around him, her knees behind his, her stomach breathing him to sleep. He pictures her large bed where she does everything, reads, eats, polishes her nails, studies chess books, talks to him on the telephone. During the first month he insisted on the formality of the couch for at least cocktails, but she sat so stiffly, as if she were still at her drafting board, that they were soon back on her bed, pillows propped against the quilted headboard although he is never entirely comfortable. It's the only detail of their affair, this cave-bed, that he has kept from his shrink. Cracker crumbs everywhere like a sandbox. Crunching — the springs like that squeak on the stairs.

Next the landing and then another short set of stairs. Big houses amaze him, like living in a hotel — everything so far away from the kitchen, a room for this, a room for that. At last he stands at the entrance of the bedroom, adjusting to this new light, letting his face cool beneath his nylon mask, turning his head from side to side. He listens for sounds of breathing in sleep. Two figures on the bed — one turned toward the far wall, the man; one flat on its back, the wife. The dresser is long and low just inside the doorway wall, the jewelry box on the far side. Maybe some things in the middle drawer. "Put your purse away," he is always telling his own wife. He can hold his breath for one minute thirty-five seconds last time Nick clocked him. He checks for shoes, junk in his path, and starts across counting as he moves past the threshold of his fear. He never uses a light.

She knows what she heard even before she sees a man appear in the doorway. She lowers her eyelids to slits, pulls air in and out of her lungs to mimic sleep. Her hand is within inches of her husband's buttocks but she can't move, or else she can't bring herself to touch him there. Slowly the shadow slides across the wall, its back to the bed, searching for her diamond ring. What else — her emerald brooch, the long rope of pearls from her mother's graduation. "No, not the pearls," she wants to cry out. "I was mother's little girl."

It was a slight change in the tone of light. He knows there is someone else in the room. Sighting down the rifle of his legs he brings the man into view. His breathing practice of countless nights keeps his body under control. He wishes he had a gun. Should he call out, reach for a lamp or phone, alert his wife by groping for her hand? But she is awake, surely she sees the figure. If she knew he lies awake beside her, it would be more evidence of his cowardliness. Her jewelry is only so much furniture anyway — just smaller.

They are both sleeping, he checked that, but there is something different about the way they sleep that nags him. As if they have been forcibly tucked in, both coiled side by side, head to toe. He moves down the dresser searching for the box. Going after three pieces listed in the rider Nick copied from the office files. A big diamond — maybe three, four carats — an emerald pin, and pearls. The pearls are lying out as if they'd just been worn. He slips them into his pocket to waiting folds of cotton gauze to muffle sound. Next, the wooden box, wooden inlaid with three drawers. He bends slightly to see more clearly. Still counting — at ninety-five seconds he will have to leave to breathe. The pin. Into his pocket. The ring — should be in the jewel box cause she doesn't wear it much, Nick said. And there it is, must be four gorgeous carats. Ba — by. Into his glove and he turns to go. "Kill him," a voice whispers. Slowly he turns to the bed, not believing his bad luck.

"It's OK," she whispers again, trying to keep her voice calm, persuasive. "Kill my husband. I'll pay tomorrow." The words come out as if they have been planned last week, last year, rehearsed for months. She can barely see the man turn toward her voice. Her body no longers feels attached to anything, sheets, bed. She cannot live through this moment, and then the next as he takes a step toward the bed. She breathes in, to rasp out again, "ten thousand." He comes another step closer. His features are molded by a stocking into a grotesque vegetable shape. She is going to faint. His face is a dream. "Jesus," he says, his flat lips moving like dark red worms. Eyes like the sockets of dead men. He makes no sound as he turns and goes, out the door, down the steps, not quiet now, and, she supposes wildly, keeps on going. Tears leak from her eyes, slide down to her ears, to the pillow. How would she have lived with that? She has to leave him. Why has she waited for her husband's move as a deserted warehouse begs for arson in the night? It really is the end. She has been saved.

He is disbelieving. *She said it twice.* She spoke to that dark shape as if her life depended on this one chance. He almost sees her real again, feels his heart warm to the heat of her desperation. It is the first time he has respected hate. Yet he's frozen into a target so still and ready that even now that the man is gone—although he could come back—he can't move. There could have been that stocking around his neck, his tongue as thick as now and dry, but hanging out. Or blood so deep it would have floated both of them to freedom. Would she have lain and watched? How could he have taken so much for granted—like her resignation to his lies, her days, her life. He will lie here till morning, stark awake, lie here for the last time, he knows that for certain, until some morning sound sets him free. Then he will surely leave; his staying he sees now unfair to both of them. They will call the police, so their last day together will be a public one. Questions from some officer with a dull pencil and yellow pad. Did either of them see him? They will both answer "no" with averted eyes. Hear anything? Only the valuables are gone.

He is out the door in ten seconds flat not stopping for the silver. He is getting too old for this. Thought he was a goner sure as hell, but she wasn't talking to her old man lying there beside her. *She was talking to him.* He peels stocking, gloves, the cotton fingers are sticky wet, but he ditches them before he reaches the street. Je—sus. He ought to go back and give it to *her*—except it ain't his thing. He doesn't carry a gun—professionals don't need them. The car parked two blocks away seems the next country. No sirens or flashing lights yet. Did she call the police, wake her husband? Or Christ, kill her old man, laying blame. Nick'll have to fence these way out of state—it's a losing proposition. And he'll have to keep an eye to the newspapers —he don't need a murder rap. The deserted streets tempt him to speed, but he drives careful. He is too old for this. Monday he'll call his uncle, get into the hardware business for once and all. Stay home nights. Be nicer to his wife.

The Visitor

Richard drove around the block twice before he spotted a parking space across from his wife's, his ex-wife's, house. Glass snapped underneath his tires — but he could tell from the sound, a muffled crunching, that it had been driven over before. Street cleaners didn't come around much to this part of town — a run-down neighborhood in Queen Village, "on its way to gentrification" some said, pointing to new brick sidewalks, landscaped parks, and voluntary integration. But he had his doubts.

He leaned against his car door to click it gently shut. His impulse was to walk away without locking it — a '67 Chevy in the year '82 — but he remembered Joshua, his eight-year-old son, was on his third bicycle. The first had its lock cut through. The second had been stolen by a ten- or eleven-year-old kid who'd pointed a kitchen knife at Joshua's face. He locked the car.

Across the street, Kate's porch and front steps were half-scraped down and a new storm door added since he'd last been here two months ago. Large pots of red geraniums bloomed under the mailbox. Kate considered them a happy magical flower and planted or potted them within a week of her arrival in any permanent place. Their persistence made him nervous — especially when she brought them indoors for winter.

He climbed the steps and knocked, feeling shy. A child came clambering down from the second floor — probably Joshua. Elizabeth, at eleven, no longer clumped — she strolled downstairs, glided into rooms when she remembered to.

"Oh, Dad. Hi." Joshua pulled the door open then gave him a fierce squeeze around the waist. Joshua was a thin child whose strength always surprised Richard. His freckles, millions of them, made him seem vulnerable. Richard tousled his son's blond hair, getting sand under his fingernails. He had the distinct feeling that Joshua had been waiting for someone else, even though Richard had made an appointment with Kate to pick up his books from Stanford days. Made an appointment. What a way to think about seeing his own kids. But he rarely saw them here. Kate usually dropped them by his place every other weekend. Sometimes he picked them up at school where they waited standing by the fence with their overnight bags — Joshua with one of his old gym bags and Elizabeth's in the shape of skates. But made an appointment — it clotted his throat when he thought about it. When he missed them at nights too quiet for office work or reading. When he splashed ketchup on his solitary scrambled eggs. "A terrible habit the kids picked up from you," Kate once said.

"Come on in." Joshua moved into their part of the house, past coats and boots in the newly painted front hallway. Once again it reminded Richard of Kate's ability to build something out of nothing while he read another book. They had separated two years ago when he had left her in Oregon and eventually both migrated back to Philadelphia — old scenes for her, more school for him. They had taken run-down apartments in the sadder parts of town, but in the pattern of their marriage she had immediately found an editing job and turned a tiny advance from a children's book into a down payment on this old townhouse. Now, each time he came, something new had been done: the painted woodwork stripped, sanded, and oiled; bookshelves built in the living room. Today it was a new mantelpiece. Probably dragged a mile from someone's junk pile.

He followed Joshua through the living room, dining room, and into the kitchen where Kate was chopping vegetables at an old oak desk she used instead of a counter. She was short and could do it comfortably; its height had always hurt his back, the few times he had cooked in the Oregon kitchen.

"Want some coffee? Just made," Kate said.

"Sure." He didn't, but he appreciated her gesture.

"One minute," she said, pushing her granny glasses up on her nose. She was prettier without them. Her blonde hair was pulled back by a rubber band decorated with two glass balls like small marbles; they must be Elizabeth's. Kate never wore lipstick now although he liked her in lipstick. In fact, he liked her. But he knew they would never live together again, although they occasionally made love. She cried afterward while washing up, the spigot on full force so he wouldn't hear. Him lying in their old bed, looking around the room at strangely familiar things like lamps, pictures they had chosen together, her silver-backed hairbrush from her grandmother. He needed her, but he didn't love her. She loved him, but she didn't need him. It had just worked out that way.

"Where's Elizabeth?" He sat down at the round table with the Indian cloth while Kate turned on the burner under the coffee. They both busied themselves during greetings, avoiding the awkwardness of the absent kiss.

"She'll be down," Kate said, but she wiped her hands on her apron and went to the hall steps to call "Elizabeth, your father's here." Wiping her hands seemed a strangely vulnerable gesture to him — her only one. She probably was unaware of how affecting he found it.

Noisily, Joshua poured himself a too-full glass of milk, looked around for the cookie jar.

Elizabeth came softly down the stairs and slid into the kitchen. Her arm, held stiffly out from her body, was encased in a white plaster cast.

"What did you do to your arm?" Richard stood up fast, upsetting the ladder-back chair he'd always hated.

"Broke it," Elizabeth said, stopping abruptly by the archway. Her curly hair was being straightened by five clip pins on either side of her pale face. Her green eyes were wide open, her lips parted, trying to look as wounded as possible.

"Broke it! Why the hell wasn't I called? What did the doctor say?" At the stove Kate turned her back and was pouring coffee into two mugs decorated with copulating rabbits. Elizabeth came over to him and gave him a hug with her other arm.

"Oh, it'll get better," Elizabeth said, shrugging her free shoulder.

"But Lizzie, Elizabeth. How did it happen?" Richard pictured neighborhood punks in obscene tee shirts following her home from

school, pushing her bicycle, knocking her down. He breathed deeply, fluttering her hair. "Jesus, Kate. You should have called me." He
forced himself to hold Elizabeth gently in arms that wanted to
strangle his wife. "Don't I count for anything? Her father," yelling
now, "just because I don't live here..."

Giggles bubbled down into Joshua's milk like fish.

"OK, kids. That's enough," Kate said. "Tell him."

Richard turned Elizabeth around to face him. "Show me where it's
broken."

Joshua's giggles turned into a coughing fit. Kate put a steaming
cup of coffee down in front of Richard before she could pat Joshua's
heaving back. His freckles grew pale against the redness of his face
and neck.

"Shut up," Elizabeth whirled around to face her brother. She
pulled away from Richard and raised her arm that was in the cast and
hit Joshua over the head. "You ruin everything."

"It's a fake!" Joshua exploded, cowering beneath his raised arms.
"It's a fake break!"

"Mom, make him shut up." Elizabeth raised the cast again as
Joshua ducked.

"Joshua, let Elizabeth..." Kate started.

"What's going on?" Richard retrieved the chair he'd knocked over
and slammed it down hard on the floor. His hands would tremble if
he let go of it.

"Stop it. Your father's only here a short time." Kate's eyes were
tearful from the onions on the chopping board.

Richard watched as Elizabeth unwrapped the strips of white cloth
from the cast. He felt the terror of a parent whose child was in
danger, the terror also of being left out. If it had been for real, Kate
would have called him. But he didn't know that for sure. And he
couldn't bring himself to ask. He had already asked it.

"See," Elizabeth held out half a cast to him, hollow on the inside.
"You have to wrap something around it to keep it on." She waved
strips of white gauze, the ruse of surrender. "Turkey-basting stuff.
Mom wrapped it really good."

"Really well," Richard said. He sat down, a damn yo-yo.

"Come on," Kate said. "It's a joke." Her teeth kept her bottom lip from following the top into a smile.

"Nick's bringing me something next time," Joshua said.

"And I'm going to spoil it for you, too." Elizabeth kicked at him as Joshua grabbed for the cast.

"Who's Nick?" Richard asked, instantly regretting it because he didn't want Kate to think him jealous.

"He sells magic," Joshua said.

"He lives upstairs," Elizabeth said. "He's our second boarder, came after Mr. Murchie moved in. Here, let me give you a broken arm."

"I don't want a broken arm." But she pulled his arm from behind his back, crooked it at the elbow to just above the belt. She began wrapping it, her tongue caught between her teeth, big teeth like his own, but her mother's gesture. The telephone rang. "I'm bringing soup," Kate said to someone, glancing back at the pile of vegetables on the desk. "Don't worry, the kids eat anything." Elizabeth rolled her eyes at Richard.

When they were married, Kate often called another couple or family to come over for a fast meal and get together. They had some of the strangest combinations of food: Kate's spaghetti with the Murphys' clam chowder and corn pudding; tacos, fried chicken wings in sweet and sour sauce, and cherry jello salad. Chaotic dinners where something always spilled, a colorful liquid dripping through the crack in the center of the table to the floor. He'd been annoyed, then, mopping up on hands and knees, but now he missed the bustle of life Kate and the children led. It went right on without him. Why was he so surprised?

"Bread too," Kate said into the phone. "And I'll pick up some wine."

They were going out to dinner. Another pot-rot-luck, as Joshua called it. So Richard wouldn't be staying to dinner tonight, or sleeping over. He realized now that he'd been counting on it. Maybe this was Kate's way of pulling free. She knew he was coming. "Bye," she hung up and went back to her desk.

"How did the ad go?" he asked her, sipping his coffee, careful not

to drip on the white wrapped case he clutched to his stomach like a shield.

"Great, I got about twenty calls right off," she said studying her herb shelf, choosing two. "Three people looked at the room. Mr. Murchie was the second and Nick the third. The first guy wanted meals, but I'm not ready to run a boarding house. The basement went fast too." She told him about the young couple downstairs, the woman a research nurse and her husband in computer science and going for a Ph.D. at Drexel. Mr. Murchie ran the movie projector at the movie theater nearby. A widower for twenty years. Nick sold magic to magic shops. He had the Delaware Valley territory.

"How can someone make a living selling tricks? Anyway, I thought all magicians bought their stuff in New York. Needed certification to even get into one of those stores."

"They probably do," Kate said. "This is joke store stuff," she pointed her knife at his broken arm. "You know. Like that thing."

"Really neat stuff; you should see his suitcases. Nickels with nails through them to pound into the floors. Itching powder," Joshua scratched his ribs elaborately.

"Plastic dog-do," Elizabeth said.

A door slammed, rattling the kitchen windows. "He's home," Joshua's chair scraped back and he ran into the hall. "Hey, Nick, what'd you bring me?"

They couldn't hear what Nick said, but his footsteps preceded Joshua's. Then, "Kate, you home?"

"Back here," Kate called, pushing her glasses up as Nick burst through the doorway, then stopped dramatically, his hand to his heart. Joshua danced up and down behind him.

"Hey, mister, you got a broken arm or something?" Nick said, winking at Richard. Do people really wink any more?

"Oh, Nick," Elizabeth giggled and gave him a push. "You know he doesn't. But the gauze makes it look real."

"This is my husband, Richard — my ex-husband," Kate corrected.

"Pleased to meet you," Nick said, coming around the table and knocking twice on the cast with his knuckles. He had a thin face between ears that protruded at a good sixty-degree angle from his head. He wore a black shirt with pearl buttons, chino pants, and a suede

jacket, and reminded Richard of the man who runs the duck shoot at carnivals. Richard wished he could see his shoes. The image faded quickly as Nick smiled — an open country smile, big, broad, and full of slightly crooked teeth. Richard nodded, bumping his nose on the coffee mug.

"Show Dad the penny trick," Joshua said as he pulled at Nick's jacket in the back. Nick swatted behind him, missing Joshua by two feet.

"Not now, not now." Nick was digging into a battered wallet held together by a thick rubber band. He pulled out two crisp twenties and snapped them on the desk next to the chopped carrots. "Another week of tricks," he said, rolling his eyes faster than Richard thought possible. Joshua immediately practiced rolling his.

"Dad, get a penny out," Elizabeth commanded, her hand out. "He'll do it," she assured her father. Richard suspected he would. Kate resumed castrating the vegetables with her favorite knife.

Nick stood, hands on his hips, feet spread wide in dark red cowboy boots. "Can I keep the penny? Only fair!"

"Da — ad." Elizabeth shook her outstretched hand, recently broken, miraculously recovered. Richard found a penny, grateful for small favors, and handed it over to Elizabeth who whirled and flipped it back to Nick. He twirled once fast before he caught it. They must have done this bit before, Richard thought, hunching forward, wishing he could ignore the stage.

"Now watch close," Joshua said, backing up to Richard's chair.

Nick held the penny for all to see, requiring Richard to nod, and then proceeded to lose it and find it in Joshua's ear, Elizabeth's collar, chanting "now you see it, now you don't," just like the three-card monte guys squatting over their bent cards in Washington Square. Nick lost it in the carrots, "Thank God it didn't get into the onions," found it in his boot, held his arms wide, his buttons gleaming in the light, and made the penny go from one hand to another. Richard couldn't follow it at all. Finally, the penny ended up in Nick's pocket just where he said it would. Richard felt a mild surprise.

"Thank you. Thank you." Nick bowed low to the children's applause, Kate clapped too. Richard tapped on his cast.

"More," Joshua shouted, jumping up and down.

"That'd cost another penny. Might break the bank," Nick said, his eyes wide, seeming to move nearer to his ears.

Annoyed, Richard started digging around for another penny.

"Nope, no more," Nick said.

"You said you'd bring Joshua something this time," Elizabeth informed Nick, her hands on her bony little hips. "What'd you bring him?"

"Hey, Lizzie. I bring something for you, you get it. I bring something for Josh, he gets it. Got it?" Josh preened. Richard was amazed that Elizabeth didn't correct Nick for calling her "Lizzie."

"Cup of coffee?" Kate offered Nick, avoiding Richard's eyes.

"Lord, no. When I drink coffee, it means I'm on the road. And tonight I'm off. Got me a date, and in another hour I'm going to have me the first beer of the night." He actually snapped his fingers. Richard's own fingers tingled as if they had fallen asleep, the cast wrapped too tightly. In fact, he no longer felt his arm now lying in his lap like a white zucchini. Richard began to unwrap it.

"Well, when do I get my present?" Josh asked.

"Better show him fast. I want to at least see it before he breaks it," the new Lizzie pouted. Her hair clips had disappeared.

Nick took each child by the ear. "Hey, I just got in from a hard week. Gimme a break. But not that kind." He nodded at Richard's dismantled cast. His large ears moved when he winked again. "Tell you what. I'm going to put my stuff upstairs and take a shower. You come up in about half an hour, OK." When he let go of their ears, Elizabeth touched hers immediately. "I'll whistle down." They all nodded — even Richard. The kids followed Nick to the stairs.

So I have half an hour, Richard thought sourly. He put the cast on the table. Kate picked up the two twenties from the desk and put them into her apron pocket, an apron he'd given her for Valentine's Day five years ago. Her aprons always seemed quaint. He didn't know other women who wore them. Kate gave him a sidelong glance off the vegetables then scooped them up with a huge slotted spoon and plopped them into the pot. This was so much a portrait of their past — him sitting at the old table while she cooked. Keeping her company as she kneaded bread, rolled out pie crusts, melted wax for jelly jars. Sometimes reading to her or calling out crossword clues. Not doing magic tricks, for sure.

"Nice guy," Richard said. "Good playmate for the kids. I'll have to take some lessons."

"Pays the mortgage," Kate said.

"All those pennies, must take him a while."

"You have to admit he's good. The kids love it."

"Good influence. Neat dresser —"

"Don't be such a prig." Kate turned her back to him as the kids returned.

"I'm going to be a magician," Joshua said. "They make lots of money. And travel all over the world."

"You're too clumsy," Elizabeth said.

"You suck!"

"Enough! Get your school papers to show your father." They had become your father and your mother almost entirely now. Meat was sizzling in a kettle. Kate poured water on top and stirred the vegetables some more.

"You ever hear of Dini?" Joshua asked.

"Hou — dini," Elizabeth said, scattering bits of chewed cookie over the table.

"Yuck," Joshua gagged.

"Everyone knows about Houdini," Richard said wiping up cookie crumbs with his napkin. "He was a master magician. But some of the things that scientists did were thought to be magic too, or witchcraft. Like Louis Pasteur. Maybe you'll be a scientist like him. He discovered..."

"Nope, I'm going to be a magician," Joshua said shaking his head. Richard wanted to give him a swipe.

The telephone rang again, and Kate cajoled a plasterer into coming early next week to fill the holes in her ceilings. The week she moved in she spent the first three evenings after work tearing out the old acoustical tiles with the Beatles' "Sergeant Pepper's" album turned up full volume — the only one unpacked. "Couldn't you have lived with those fake ceilings till you got settled in?" Richard had asked, his first visit, wading through three feet of crumbled ceiling, as he had waded before through shredded wallpaper, fields of cut weeds.

"Nope," she said from high on the ladder. "Don't worry, it's nothing you're going to have to help with." And it was true he found her energy unnerving. When they had finally separated he had been relieved that he could abdicate at last from all her projects with no guilt. His apartment had no projects. He couldn't say for sure what color the walls were — beige? yellow? For Kate they would be the wrong color, but she had never been to his apartment, at least inside. He never asked her. Once she had appeared at his door, late, when he had friends there — and his girl friend. Not the one he'd been seeing when he left Kate. He'd talked with Kate a while on the steps telling her he wasn't coming back to her. She'd been drinking. She had looked odd at first without her apron, unclothed in some erotic way. "I painted three rooms today," she'd blubbered, "rolled it on. All white." Tiny paint spots had gleamed in her hair.

"Jo — sh," a young boy's voice accompanied a knocking at the door. Josh called that he was in the kitchen. "It's Larry," he said to Richard.

Larry stopped in the doorway, his chubby arm draped over a slightly deflated soccer ball resting on his hip. He nodded uncertainly to Richard. "I'm the father," Richard wanted to say, but it was too foolish.

"We're leaving soon, so don't make any plans," Kate's head was inside the refrigerator. Steam came out with her voice. She straightened up, "And anyway, your father is here to see you."

Larry glanced at Richard, probably to see what a father looked like, Richard thought, immediately annoyed with himself for thinking in clichés about a black family. Larry's father was probably home this minute sanding floors or putting in some cozy patio.

"That's my Dad," Joshua said, hooking his thumb at Richard. Larry said "Hi."

They all heard Nick's whistle. With two fingers, Richard was sure.

"That's Nick," Joshua punched the ball off Larry's hip. "Come on, he'll show you too. Hey, we should have a magic club." They ran out and up two flights to the third floor as Kate followed them calling to come back down in five minutes because their father had come to see them, not her. Sadly, Richard realized that their intermittent appearances of the last few minutes pleased him, were more normal than the weekend visits to his apartment when each of their individual lives went on hold. He remembered them perched on the edge of his new couch their first visit. "Well?" hung in the air — to their credit, unsaid. Activities bumped along from movies and zoos to dinner to TV, with no flow or intermingling with friends or the slow chopping of vegetables for soup. He had no room like Kate's kitchen where she could always be found, and therefore left. Was that why he could leave her? Sad for them both.

Another knock and Kate returned with a young woman in a white uniform sprinkled with irregular dark brown spots.

"This is Shirley. Lives downstairs." Shirley nodded and sat down across from Richard, obviously at home. She at least seemed to know who he was. Kate poured her a mug of coffee while Shirley told them about a lawsuit being brought against an anesthesiologist at her hospital. A young girl had been operated on for a spinal problem and her head had been unsupported under the sheet. When she woke she was paralyzed on her right side. How could a parent survive something happening to a child, Richard thought, remembering the shock of Elizabeth's white cast. Except that maybe one of the tragedies of being a parent is learning to survive even that. Shirley blew into her cup, her eyes bright from a tale well told, waiting for some comment. Richard tilted back in his chair, damned if he'd say anything. Just then the kids came thundering down the stairs, but they passed on through and outside, shouting and banging on the wall.

Soup steamed away on the stove. Kate took off her apron and hung it on a peg. She wrapped tinfoil around a fresh loaf of bread and put it in a shopping bag. Richard swallowed the extra saliva in his mouth. He stood up and pushed his chair tightly into the table as if to save his place.

"I think I'll be going along," he said.

"Can you imagine how those parents felt?" Shirley said, shaking her head.

Richard moved into the living room and waited for Kate to follow. He didn't say goodbye to Shirley, bearer of impersonal bad news.

"I'll come by some other time for the books," he said. "And I'll skip meeting Mr. Murchie this time." He jerked his head toward the kitchen. "And Mr. Shirley." Kate didn't answer him. This is your choice, her eyes told him. Yes—it was. She turned away to the window as if watching for the kids, but also to avoid any contact of good-bye. Her wide hips tempted him to move in close behind, to press himself against her. He would have liked to stay over tonight, to sleep within the shadow of the old oak headboard, to imagine soup still bubbling below, but he started toward the door instead, kicking aside a pair of kids' boots.

"Maybe Mr. Murchie can get the kids in free to some R-rated movies. Or they can be movie ushers," he said, feeling mean.

"G," she said, angrily. "Just G."

Six or seven kids were playing a quasi-soccer game when Richard came out.

"It's Dad," Joshua yelled giving the ball a last hard kick. They all gathered noisily at the foot of the steps, Elizabeth elbowing her way to the front. Still his kids, they were. Still his.

"You leaving?" Joshua asked, panting. He tapped Richard on the arm four or five times although he already had his attention.

"Well. . ." He was willing to be talked into staying a little longer. Play a little soccer till they had to leave with their mother and the bread and the soup.

"Course he's leaving," Elizabeth said, giving Joshua a push. She too patted Richard's arm. His body felt sensitized to their slightest touch at these leave-takings.

"Are you going, mister?" a red-headed boy asked, bouncing his ball impatiently.

And so he kissed them good-bye, their faces sandy with sweat and dust.

"See you this weekend." He'd take them to a real park where they could play soccer on grass. Maybe take Larry too. He got into his car and slammed the door, forgetting its fragile nature. They wrote messages on the dusty fenders that he would read later. He rolled down his window and Elizabeth leaned in for a last squeeze. He hated this moment more than any other, their limp waves, sometimes their game already begun before he was out of the parking space.

"Come back again sometime," Joshua called, echoing his mother's line to departing guests. Dear Joshua couldn't know the damage that phrase could do. Richard waved and rolled the window back up. The car slid over the glass into the street, holding together, but now accompanied by a long high whine. And he'd just had it in the garage for repairs. He caught a glimpse of the kids in his rearview mirror as he turned onto Passyunk Avenue. They were all standing out in the street waving vigorously, yelling good-byes. Tears welled up in his eyes. If only he could move into one of Kate's upstairs rooms. Be a good friend to her, bring things to the kids. Have his meals with them. Sometimes he ached for them as a family. He'd close his eyes and conjure up the mess, the noise.

A couple of blocks later the metallic scream began to drive him crazy with its seriousness. He pulled up to the open doors of a garage and hastily wiped his eyes. A young mechanic had Richard gun the motor several times, then motioned for him to pull forward onto the rack. The high sound gained momentum then whined away as Richard stopped the car on the two treads. He got out and the hydraulic lift whooshed into action. The car rose slowly, its body trimmed in rusty lace.

"Ain't exactly heard that before," the young man said. He pushed his long hair back beneath his cap, then ducked under the car. Richard followed gingerly, watching him poke around the muffler. Finally he extracted a little round disc from the exhaust. He turned it over twice. "Gotta be kidding," he said.

Richard pictured a broken, irreplaceable part.

"You had a joke played on you, mister," the mechanic said, holding out the greasy disc to Richard. "Some smart-ass kids wanting to give you a loud send-off." He laughed, pushing his hat back. "See any kids hanging around when you left somewheres?"

"You mean the noise came from this thing? Somebody stuck this in my car?" It had the weight of a fifty-cent piece.

"That's what I'm telling you. It's one of them joke-shop things. Can give you a scare, car as old as this one." The car was settling slowly beside them.

Richard left there fast. He drove without purpose, the disc a lump in his pocket. This weekend Joshua would want it back — Nick's new present. And he'd want to hear the whole story, how Richard found it, the rack, the guy's face. Then he'd tell Nick and next time Richard was over visiting, Nick would wink at him. "Heard you had some car trouble," he'd say. Somehow it was only the beginning.

He opened the window and threw the disc as far as he could, listening to it ping away on the street in a feeble last sound. He remembered Joshua's and Elizabeth's faces as they watched him leave, their hands waving wildly when he turned the corner. Joshua's words trailing away, "Come back again sometime."

His throat vibrating, he heard again that high whine, almost a wail vibrating as if deep in his chest, now the cry of his own voice.

Night Walk

Feldman checks into the hotel and unpacks his two-day wardrobe. He washes his face and thinks about a steak in a red wine sauce. Then maybe a walk around the city. A night clerk in the lobby is reading a newspaper as Feldman strolls past him to the sidewalk. He remembers Gilmore's advice in the faculty lounge, "You be careful down there. Washington's white by day and black by night. Just stay inside after dark." Gilmore is the type who utters judgments on places, people, and books as if to say, "you listen to me and you needn't read it, know them, or go there." He shivers, remembering. No one listens to Gilmore but his warnings have a way of sitting in your head like a row of tin ducks in a carnival booth just waiting to be knocked over.

Tucker, you is almost done work tonight. The jukebox that usually keeps him moving is almost never playing. He should've stayed home. He feels the cold in his bones every time a customer stomps in the tavern door — which ain't often. The dishes and glasses are dribbling back, not enough to keep the washer hose busy. Pretty soon Al will be out here telling him to lay off the rest of the night just to save his self a few nickels. Leering at him like he's already seeing two black asses bumping and rooting behind his eyes. Seeing all blacks as big bucks. There will come a time he'll be asking for a piece. His way of integrating. And Tucker'll tell him, "I'll see." That's just what he'll tell him.

When Feldman finds a restaurant six blocks away, his collar is up and his hands are deep inside his pockets. The steak is thick, though sauceless. A half-bottle of red wine takes the chill off the night. He misses his wife. They spend most evenings reading together, comfortably apart. He tells the waiter no dessert. The restaurant is almost empty. Somebody likes Bach. He has a final coffee. He can eat steak alone but dessert needs company. He'll take a walk.

Al is telling his same old jokes. Tucker stands there listening to the drunks laughing. He wishes someone would put a quarter in the box. Two plates and three glasses come back for washing, which don't take Tucker longer than a minute. When Al's head appears in the square window between the kitchen and bar Tucker starts rolling down his sleeves. "Hey, Tucker, might as well lay off here and get some laying done early tonight," Al calls. The drunks laugh. Tucker salutes him and hangs up his half-dirty apron to dry. His silver cuff links are on the window ledge. He lifts them wide of the drain and threads them through his cuffs. Then he puts on his new red sport coat and stands in front of the washroom mirror admiring the match with his pink and rose striped shirt. A mean dude, he says, cocking his flat-brimmed hat down over his left eye. Tucker, you's a real dude. He bums a pack of cigarettes from Rosie, gives the bird to Al's whistle, and leaves wishing some music was leading the way.

Outside the restaurant Feldman looks up and down the street, deciding which way to start walking. A chauffeured car sucks an elderly couple from under the canopy, north toward Capitol Hill. Another solitary diner nods at him vaguely, going in the opposite direction. He puts his collar up again. He's cold but he wants to make the most of his time — look around a bit. And considering what he has to say to the government bunch tomorrow he'll probably not be invited back. It isn't his idea of a vacation spot. A few cars are running solos on the deserted streets. Mostly taxis. All taken. The blocks of sidewalk stretch ahead into larger city blocks. Stretch to a bright red blur coming his way. He starts off.

Too cool, Tucker's bones tell him. It is one hell of a cool night. But Sadie'll be warm. He blows hot air into his hands. Ain't no use thinking cold if he ain't going to be warm them ten blocks to home. Flashes of pink and rose keep him moving from store window to store window. Sadie likes red. She'll be just waking up when he gets there. "Whitey should pay for that housework in blood," she says when she comes home from work. Sleep gets her good humors back. She'll say, "Ooooooh, man, look at you." He is striding long. His collar is up for now. His fingers are in the slim flat pockets. Not the thumbs, gotta keep this jacket smooth, man. Gotta think warm. Gotta stomp hard. Boots coming down hard on cold cement — like gunshots — couple of night noises to keep the rats guessing.

That outfit'd shake up the dean, Feldman thinks, as a red jacket brings a rose and pink shirt a little nearer. A hat his son would save his allowance for. But Gilmore would call out the National Guard. He admires the long body, the loose jaunty stride. His own steps make little noise.

Shoulda worn me a coat tonight. Shoulda bought me a dude coat with wide shoulders, a belt, big brass buttons. Tucker slips his thumbs into the pockets still flat. There'll be some warming to do before the loving begins. He'll tell Sadie, "Stay right where you are," moving her over a little, making room for him. Shoulda called in to Al that he was staying home. Ain't no one out tonight. Except for dumb tourists like the one down the street a way. Gawking around looking for the president.

It's the wine, Feldman thinks, listening. He sees wine-red shoulders, hidden hands. Long legs, a black face under a wide brim. When the man's eyes come into range he wants to look away. He must be cold in that thin red jacket without a coat. His *boots* are making that noise.

Hey white man, you out of your territory. The president don't come down here. Maybe you is looking for some natives. Well you is seeing Tucker who is one cool dude. You look hard, you hear. He wouldn't be caught dead in that hair-bone coat. But it sure looks warm and Tucker ain't. And that coat shouldn't be here. Ain't no one told this whitey night ain't his time. The U.S. government is a day-time oper-a-tion.

Feldman hates himself as soon as the thought occurs to him, but it doesn't go away. Is he going to pass him on the left or on the right? He has trouble walking. Maybe he should have stayed at the hotel. He trips over a sidewalk crack.

Shit. He's seen that look before. Whitey's a block away looking two blocks past him as if he, Tucker, ain't wearing the meanest threads he owns. As if he ain't even here on the street. Tucker sees him hesitate and stumble. Whatever you get out here you got it coming to you man. He warms to a game. He slants left, then right, then left. Sure, he'll do a dance for the man.

His sweat is cold on his face. He can hear Gilmore saying, "Fancy a bleeding-heart liberal dying like that." But two degrees to the right is the wrong turn because the man swerves too. Eagerly Feldman moves to the left as if waving a white flag. Then slipping in his sweat he turns right again. He loves this man in his red jacket and his pink-striped shirt. His chest aches with love. He is afraid to die. But he will understand.

Tucker feels almost warm weaving toward the man. Keeping him guessing. Suddenly he knows the pull of temptation. He can't be letting this one get away. The air dries his teeth inside his grin.

At fifteen feet Feldman's lungs expand. His muscles tighten into traps which sever both his legs. He stands, finally, and waits.

Man, you is scared shitless. Of little ol' Tucker. Ain't seen one so white for days. Now what'll it be? A quick jab to the gut. Or maybe just a clean slice from ear to ear.

He's cold from the sweat and wet from the piss running down his legs. Feldman holds out his hands in a gesture he doesn't understand. The man's crazy. The world's crazy.

Tucker is in the air. Warm. He lands like gunshots in front of the man and he yells, high, to wake the dead. He yells, "Boo." Then he is laughing fit to kill. He is holding his stomach, his pink shirt, his red jacket, to keep from dying. Sadie, you has missed it. Ba—by.

Then Feldman is laughing too, his mouth still rubbery. He reaches out for the red jacket, they are both laughing. His arms are out and Tucker takes them in. Tucker is warmed by the heavy coat and they are both laughing until they cry.

The Sorting Out

1

I missed it, I think. Never was much at counting. Back or forth. Always depended on Ma for that ever since it started up then down my legs that time we were buying new flowered oilcloth in the dry-goods store. Maybe it was towels.

2

I missed it again, Ma thinks this time. Easier having Ma think. Pa don't much. Just sits at the round kitchen table after coming home from the swing shift at the mill. Drinks his beer cursing the farm and the taxes and the strip mines making patterns on the land back over our hill. We eat our big meal at noon before he goes to work. Ma peels potatoes every day. "This month went fast," she says over the potatoes. I set three plates on the table. We both can see Pa out by the barn throwing corn for the hens. "You ain't had your visitor this month yet." I think about the silent, wet visitor I don't much like. "Not yet," I say.

3

The third time I am sick in the morning in the basin by the back door, Ma clears me out of the kitchen fast. But not fast enough, cause I hear Pa calling her back. And then I don't hear no more as I dive head first for the pillow on my bed. And then I feel his footsteps clumping down the hall and he is standing there. I can feel him standing there and he says, "OK, who was it?" and I just lay there pulling the air through the feathers. Afraid to turn over. "Who?" he yells again. He pounds his fist against the door frame, twice. "Do you know who? Going out behind my back to the fire hall and even them roadhouses I'll bet, and then out to the dump with every Tom, Dick, and Harry, and your Ma not stopping you, but knowing all along." And I think Tom, Dick, Harry, Lefty, Earl, Hal, Willie, is that all I think, but I don't say because somehow I know he wants a name, one name. Like the one he give Ma. And I think about one name but somehow their faces come floating back all together, no one stepping forward to wave — only floating by like in a parade, some with a six-pack under their arm, some a half-pint bottle. Those times when we're at the dump I throw the empty bottles at whatever I can see. The side of an old icebox, rusted bed springs, a rungless chair. I am a good aim. But this too I don't turn over and tell Pa. His fist hits the door again and then my bed is tilting like a seesaw and Ma is smoothing back my hair. "Leave her alone for now," she says. "It'll all come out soon enough." It will? I think. Her words are a comfort for now.

4

I don't go to the fire hall no more. I mean go in. Sometimes I say to Ma I'm going for a walk and she says don't be long and that is all. I go out walking. I walk up the hill, past the fire hall. I look at the cars and trucks parked on the gravel and I put drivers in them cars and trucks. Hal in the old green Dodge, Lefty in the De Soto with the rusted running boards about to fall off. Then I put myself in with the guys one at a time. I move around a bit from front to back seats. Old wool blankets under the stars. Even change the weather though in April it was mostly rain. The months stretch behind me into two or three years since I been in school and April seems like a silly word I've been thinking on too long. Like apple. Except Pa didn't mention to think about apples only April cause he counted back on the calendar. I walk slow. I miss the guys and my cousin Jennie who used to come along on double dates sometimes. I move my tongue around my mouth and try to taste sour grape wine or potato whiskey. Gin? But

nothing comes back. I miss the talk too. Just talk I used to listen to.
Laugh sometimes. Ma talks more now and I like that. Making plans.
My plans are making themselves and soon I'll be wearing the two new
dresses Ma made from the flour sacks she was saving. The side door
of the fire hall opens and music and talk comes out with the light.
Johnnie the bartender is bringing out a box of garbage and calls to
me. "Ain't seen you in a while, Ellie, where you been?" He stands
waiting so I walk over. "Oh around," I say. It ain't a lie. But there
seems to be some other truth somewhere too. "Your Pa was up here a
few weeks ago on a Saturday night asking questions." I can see him
sitting up here, having one beer. Wanting to look around at the faces
but not looking anywhere but at Johnnie and him not long. "I
couldn't tell him anything. I mean what did he want me to say?" He
squints at me in the dim light. I push a rusted can back toward the
bin. "You ain't got yourself in trouble have you, Ellie?" "Oh no," I
tell him. Him hearing one thing and me thinking "trouble." No, not
trouble. Just something different. Like a new season coming on. Not
a new season. A new time. But I wouldn't call it trouble. "I probably
won't be back," I say. Adding "for a while." Adding it for him. And
suddenly I see the new time being filled with diapers, and washings,
and bottles, and small gurgling sounds, and baking bread in between. All warm. Me and the baby. "I gotta be going," I say. "Say
hello to your Ma," he says and waves. Then he starts looking around
for an empty box to take back inside. I go back down the hill to home
where Pa would be waiting if he was home. Except I guess I wouldn't
have been gone out walking.

5

It moved. I can feel it moving inside of me. Ma knows it's moving too
cause all the sudden I go silent and feeling and pretty soon Ma is
silent too. I put my hands on my stomach as if I were resting them
there before kneading the bread again. But I'm pushing, gently, gently. Hoping it will move again. I feel myself drifting off behind my
eyes as if everything I see is in the tips of my fingers pressing in. Pa
sees too. "God damn," he says, "do I have to sit here and—" He
doesn't finish but reaches across the table and slaps me hard on the

face. I start to cry but I don't move my hands from what they're holding. Then he sits there staring. "You gotta think, girl," he says. "Put your hands in *the other place and think.*" Ma crosses to me fast and puts her hands on my shoulders, I can smell the flour. "That's enough of that talk. I've said before, 'it'll come out soon enough.' If you're sure you really want to know." Her voice is low and shaking. And then she moves to the table and leans down and speaks into his face, "You ever think of that."

6

This morning I put on the same dress I been wearing every other day for the past month. I figured it out. And every other day washing the other and hanging it to dry. As usual, Ma and I do the bread for Elmer's store at the foot of the hill. Twelve loaves every day ever since I left school somewhere around the seventh grade. Just as well as I was having trouble keeping my mind on grades and rooms and books, not having the boards to wash or the erasers to clean like in the lower grades. Ma needed company too, I think. I keep her company most mornings when we bake bread, filling the kitchen with a smell that makes us both happy. Pa still sleeping, snoring loud, later complaining that he's a farmer through and through and don't sleep a wink past five. We know better but we don't say. He ain't a farmer anymore since the strip mines come buying up the land, maybe *wishes* he was. He works late and hard but still he says it every morning somewhere around ten o'clock. We finish early today cause Pa's sister is coming to visit. I sit waiting in my room and open my closet door. In my mind I put on my clothes, it's the only place they fit anymore, so I picture them there, trying to put other things together too. That has to be the week, Pa said, standing in front of the calendar from the feed store. Looking at April, though now it's September. So I close my eyes and put on my blue dress with the red rickrack sewed on just above the hem. The dress that used to catch on the edge of Joe's car seat, or Harry's when he had the truck, after going to the fire hall or maybe even Winkle's Inn that night. I try to remember. Then I put on the white blouse that Hal buttons down the front slowly, the yellow blouse that Hal too buttons up the back cause that one I can't reach, the skirt I wear with both — either down or bunched around my middle when Hal or Harry or Willie is making me feel good before he does. "Who did it?" Pa asks again before Aunt Minnie arrives, as if he wants to make her a present of the name. His sister visits more now. She lives over Elmer's store. Gets a loaf of bread free twice a week from us. She comes over, huffing up the steps, moving her large body into position at the kitchen table. "Out running around like your Ma used to do," she says today when Ma goes to the root cellar for canned beans. I think running is not what she means. "So what's new," she asks as Ma is coming up the cellar steps. She looks at me hard wanting to know more too. But not "who," I think, she wants to know "how."

7

Pa looks older. There's a sagging to his shoulders I'd like to see stopped, but I don't have the right words just now. Ma looks younger. Is that possible? We spend the afternoons making baby clothes. We spend the money we make from baking extra loaves of bread, some fancy rolls. I hold a nightshirt up. "That small?" I say. And then I put my hands on my belly that feels that large already. "That small," Ma says and smiles. Yes, she does look younger. Like how she must have looked when she had me. But only once because I am *it,* I'm all they had. "Sons would have helped," Pa used to say. "Lord knows why no more come." It is Saturday night and Pa is on his third beer when a car pulls into the driveway. Ma goes to the door, "It's Harry Burke," she says. Pa is scraping back his chair. "Just stay where you are," Ma tells him, "He'll be along, if he got this far." We hear footsteps and then she opens the door and lets him in. I say "Hi, Harry," but that's all, I like Harry but no more no less than Hal and Lefty and Frank. But I don't run through all the names just now cause I too am wondering what he is going to say. He is wearing his sky-blue drinking shirt I used to call it. He looks good too. Been growing a mustache since I been away. But "away" don't rightly fit so I quit thinking and start listening. Ma offers him a beer but he shakes his head "no." "I been thinking," he says, sitting down at the table across from Pa, "I been thinking that maybe it's. . ." He stops and I think "maybe it's what" — "yours" — it seems a strange idea to think it belongs to more than a name. Harry clears his throat to begin again. "I been thinking maybe it is time to settle down. Get Married." "When?" Pa says. He has hooked his thumbs in his suspenders and is leaning back in his chair. Harry looks surprised. "Anytime. Now." And Ma says, "You working?" and he nods "yes," but not using much space for that movement. Then Ma says, "Settle down where?" and Harry again looks surprised, and then says, "Here." We all look around at "here" and I put myself in my bedroom and look around there too. At the double bed I fit into just fine. At my mirror. And Pa says, "So now it's coming out. A few months late. So *now* it's yours?" and Harry straightens in his chair, his hands supporting him on either side, and he says, "Well about that — how sure I got to be? I mean . . ." and Ma stands up and says in her new voice, "You got to be sure, you got to *feel* sure," and Harry shrugs and looks around at me and I nod to back up Ma. "He must know *something*," Pa says, "sure he's sure." I stand up then, careful to miss the table edge, and Harry stands up. He's thinking I'm going to say something but I don't. "I'll have to think on it," he says, puzzled I can tell. And then he is gone and Pa is pounding the table and yelling. "It would have been a *name*. It would have had a *name*." Ma pushes me into my room calling back to him, "We'll find a name." But I been looking for a name, I think, and it ain't easy.

8

Harry ain't been back though only Pa is waiting for him. I figured that myself. Ma never was waiting for anything I had to tell. We're waiting for the baby now. Sometimes in the afternoons I smooth my dress over my belly and we watch the faded flowers of the fabric move as if a wind were rippling a meadow. It's a strong one. I know that. We make it through Thanksgiving thinking our own thoughts. Pa's sister comes over and Mother's brother and wife and kids from the next town. Aunt Minnie plays a game with a string over my belly and announces that it's going to be a boy. She's wrong but I don't say. They tell me to give my feet a rest so I sit in the kitchen while they do the dishes. The men are in the front room for once. Pa is talking about other things for once too. I put my arms on my belly and drift with the baby. Just as though it's steering me somewhere. The women talk about babies. Ma says she's making an appointment for me soon with the doctor on the other side of town. Dr. Bach. Pa is sounding like his old self in the front room. The taxes this, the strip mine that. But it won't last. I would like to comfort him. But putting things together is hard. I get sleepy thinking of names, places, even songs. Like it was another world. Some other me.

9

It is all over and I am back in the room now, third bed from the end. Other beds stretching down the room a ways. Babies crying to make you smile. I am holding my baby. We are both on our backs in my bed. Ma is moving around folding things in between peeks into my bundle. Pa is here too. Sitting by the bed, his old grey hat in his hands. Sitting on the edge of his chair as if he is going to leave soon on some errand. "Well, Minnie was wrong. It's a girl," he says, and I see that old look of helplessness come back home to roost in his eyes. "It's a girl," he says again. "Go on home," Ma tells him. "You have to leave for work soon." He goes. Still wanting to know. I *do* know now — but it's not what he wants to hear. I know because I thought a lot about it. Nine months of thinking about it ever since April. Nine months of trying to put the right guy with the whiskey, beer, or wine. The right car with the right place. Me in the right clothes. And every which way I move them around it all comes back to a feeling. The bundle starts to move and cry. "She's hungry," Ma says. She helps me sit up a bit, puts a pillow behind my back. Pats us both. I pull my hospital gown aside and place my nipple near the baby's mouth. We are warm together. I watch her nose move. I touch her face. All those names fade. *Their* names. We are left together and I have given her mine.

Something to Do

One morning I wake up bored. I feel too connected with the threads of what I do, thin streamers that connect me to Boston Edison; the phone company; Saks; to the library where I have worked for four years since graduating from college; to friends who depend on me for company and I them; to old lovers wanting to be friends; to my current lover searching for a way gracefully to stop seeing me — as if I didn't know things are over long before they end.

I decide to lie.

I call my lover at his office, which automatically limits his responses. I tell him I have found someone else. I have found someone who brushes my long blonde hair, someone who reads as I read instead of pacing till I stop, who cooks elaborate breakfasts while I give myself a pedicure until the tray is actually resting on the antique quilt touching my knees, someone who does not mix his laundry in with mine. My lover is necessarily speechless as I voice some regrets. He hangs up, but I know he is torn between relief and surprise.

This has made me nervous. I always tell the truth and assume others do, too. At different times I have felt like the Statue of Liberty, the goddess Athena, Emma Goldman, Queen Victoria, although I don't know what they thought of lying. Perhaps it is the strength of their arms, one always raised on high.

I call my boss at the library and tell him the distant aunt who welcomed me into her spinster home when my parents died in a fiery plane crash, that distant aunt is ill and asking for me in New Orleans where I grew up. (It is a place I have always wanted to go.) I tell him I might be gone two weeks, that I won't know the length of my stay until I have consulted her doctor. I mention her quavering voice saying her paid companion of the past twelve years has run off with the silver and the handyman. I am expected to search for both. I will humor her, I tell my boss, but I am really going in order to be near her when she dies. The last word makes him shy so he says he will wait to hear from me. I ask that my current project be put aside, my papers put in a drawer, that it is something I'd prefer to finish myself. I can't remember what is on my desk besides the clear nail polish I wish I now had.

As I am making myself a cup of strong tea someone calls and asks for "George." This time I do not apologize for the caller's mistake. It is a woman's voice and it seems surprised by my own. I tell her George is in the shower, that he likes to take long soapy showers. I take her number, repeat it back to her, but suggest that she call again in an hour.

The phone rings once more. A friend's husband is delighted he's caught me before I've left for work. He invites me to a surprise party for his wife's thirtieth birthday. He explains it will not be tacky as so many surprise parties are. We will not be required to spring from closets or emerge from behind a couch. We will not be led in cheery singing, or shout "surprise." I tell him his taste verges on the profound, that until now no time seemed appropriate for saying so. I picture his bald head, his dome ridged like the one over the statehouse. Bald men have problems women cannot assuage. When he invites me to lunch later in the week, I accept. I name a tiny French restaurant, cozy, expensive, and so romantically lit I feel sure he will be unable to find me there. He breathes deeply, says good-bye. One always has friends one dislikes.

My best friend calls. (Not the wife of the surprise party.) She also works at the library. I take the phone and my tea into the bedroom and get comfortable. My stomach feels tight from the tension of my lies. My friend has heard "the story" about my aunt from our boss. She says "the story" because she thinks she recognizes a lie when she hears one. Maybe. I tell her I tried calling her last night. I say last week there had seemed no need to relay my worst fears to her. But now that they are realized, now that I am pregnant — I hesitate and sip my tea, allowing her to say a few nonjudgmental but soothing words of support to the effect that whatever I do she will understand. I tell her my lover and I are taking a trip that will include an abortion. It will be a bond between us, perhaps leading to the marriage I have longed for. I am annoyed that she swallows this last remark. I hold white lingerie up to my breasts and imagine an unusual wedding.

I immediately call my father to set things right. He is surprised to hear from me in daytime hours, the rates between Ohio and Boston being what they are. He says he's just about to go to the Elks for some poker. Looking out over the faces at my mother's funeral I realized that the Elks had won. He says the raccoons kept him awake all night and now what? Why Dad, I tell him, I'm just calling to say hello. I never call to say hello. His deeply suspicious nature is unable to relax into small talk, so I am forced to admit reluctantly the true reason for my call. I am annoyed by his sudden intake of breath, his certainty that I haven't failed him yet. He has already constructed various scenarios for me. He suspects I live my life to embarrass him in front of his friends. How can I disappoint him? I tell him I've decided to keep the child. "What child?" does not occur to him. The child he has been prepared for — notwithstanding that I was probably the first valedictorian of my town to hold forth on birth control at slumber parties. No, I say, you'd better sit down before I tell you about the father. I hear a kitchen chair being scraped across to the wall phone by the refrigerator. I tell him we have decided not to marry, that our relationship has been ending anyway. I imagine him only half listening, already rehearsing his role in the tragedy when I arrive home on the train (he's never flown), a wet bundle in my arms. He asks who is the father — his voice dreading the wrong race or color. That the father is unsuitable goes without saying. I feel him hoping the father is merely a married man, or an inmate of the minimum security prison he warned me against teaching furniture refinishing at, or that the father is an intelligent priest I have temporarily led astray. I announce that my lover is eschewing all legal rights to the child. I rephrase this to eliminate eschew. I say that he has decided to return to the Punjab (let him look it up) and I am taking a two-week vacation to see him off. I tell my father I love him, wishing I did. The most he'll lose today is five or ten dollars. At the Elks the stakes aren't high.

My lover calls back as I am cleaning out the refrigerator, snacking on leftovers. Now he is huddled in a phone booth trying to talk above the noise of trucks going by, and full of questions too indiscreet to utter in his office. He wants to see me but I tell him I'm not well. There is a red mold on the green beans that is the brightest I've ever seen. He demands to see me, he will be over in half an hour, but I mention I changed my locks last week when my purse was stolen on the subway. He doesn't remember my telling him this. Surely I would have told him of such a terrible thing. Perhaps this accounts. . . I cut him off lamenting his faulty memory; it is, in fact, one of the reasons I'm leaving him. "Who?" he asks. "Is it someone I know?" I realize he is behaving exactly as I might had our places been reversed. He is behaving badly. This time I hang up, tempted to tell tales of pregnancy, but I refrain.

I do not call my sister in New York. She'll be hearing from our father tonight at 11:01. I'm grateful for the ten-hour reprieve. I'll send her the first postcard. The possibilities are endless as I locate my colored pens.

My landlady beams. She promises to water the plants, which I have gathered together in my bay window, to take in my mail. She is so excited for me she wrings her hands in blessing. I'm the first person she knows to actually win something big like a trip, though her cousin used to enter all the contests and wrote jingles that were pure poetry.

I call to cancel my subscription to *Library Journal.* I tell them that somehow their computer has been sending me seventeen issues for the past three months. No doubt it is happening to others. I refrain from telling them of the new efficient filing system I have quietly instituted in the reference section of my library.

My next-door neighbor watches me pack after making us both Bloody Marys. She is sympathetic, though surprised, at my career change. She could never picture me a librarian, what with no glasses, all that blonde hair. She didn't know that Arizona State had the best veterinary school in the country. Wasn't it all snakes and bears in that area? Animals not in need of medicine? I magnanimously wave aside her lack of knowledge and show her a picture of my childhood cat. It is a photo I found last week marking someone's place in *The Annals of European Civilization.* As I fold clothes I tell her how "David Livingstone" got her name. She turns the photo over and reads "Muffy." Oh, only my crazy aunt called her that, I say.

"Getting married in New Orleans." My travel agent smiles widely. "How absolutely romantic." I mention my hesitation at meeting his parents. They are one of the prominent families always to be found at the head of the Mardi Gras parade. They live in a grand home in the disintegrating Garden District and are probably disappointed in what they've heard of me. "Not you," she says, "you'll knock them dead." I promise to try.

On the way to the airport, my cab driver practices for the Indiana 500. I tell him I feel queasy, that perhaps he should slow down, I hope I make it to a restroom. His foot jumps from the gas and he cleaves to the slow lane. "Hey, Lady, just hold on." He has another six hours' work tonight, he says, glancing back at me. I relax and promise to mention him in my prayers that evening in Paris.

Finally, fifteen minutes before boarding time, I call the police, handkerchief over the phone. I explain slowly and carefully about the bombs I have placed in the Boston Public Library. I say I have had a change of heart — they have a fighting chance with early warning. (These threats are always good for at least a half-hour coffee break.) I try to think of a signature to tip off my friends working there, to make them suspiciously thankful, but I don't want to stay on the phone. Begin in Fiction I say.

The plane seems to be waiting for me. The hostess smiles like one of my detested sorority sisters but I ignore her and incline my head to the handsome silly pilot. The gentleman dressed like a banker is sympathetic to my claustrophobia and graciously offers his window seat. I settle back remembering the day.

Sylvia

They were shadows, silhouettes, when Lynne opened the door. The man achieved color first, pale pink glazed with a half-day's growth of beard. The girl was mixed shades of brown and gray.

Lynne invited them in as the man waved a white paper. "You'll have to sign this first, Miss, and write me a check — her first week's pay. I got to get back to the city." He turned to the wall to write out the receipt, ignoring the hall table, keeping an eye on his Cadillac humming in the drive.

The girl placed two shopping bags on the floor in front of her feet and shifted an armful of papers and a worn red dictionary from one arm to another. She watched the bags, waiting.

Lynne went to the kitchen for her checkbook. She had wished for a soft, plump woman of fifty-five, a grandmotherly sort, and now she felt her vision narrow to this slim, hard girl of — nineteen.

"We guarantee she'll stay a week. Then it's between you two. Everything OK, Sylvia?"

Sylvia nodded and looked over her shoulder to the man's car. Lynne gave him the check. Silently they watched him drive away.

For the first time in months Lynne and George lingered over dinner and Sylvia cleaned up in the kitchen. The children called her black Sylvia for the first two days because they already knew a white Sylvia who lived just three houses and, Lynne thought, one world away.

June 9 1970 today is my birthday and I am thirteen years old and mama has been telling me for so long that I'm a bad girl that I almost feel it's true and I want to be a good girl for her but it's hard when all the other kids is running out and having fun and mama says it ain't just fun and I guess I know what she means because the last time we scared some whitey on the train she was a little old lady with a face like the underside of pizza dough and I wasn't just sure what junebug would do when she only give us thirty-five cents crying and wailing that she didn't have no more and lord have mercy on her soul.

When the agency check arrived with Lynne's bank statement three weeks later, Sylvia was still there. Still waiting but no longer watching. They had passed the crisis in the second week.

Sylvia had complained about a sore on her back. A red bruise, almost a wound, covered her shoulder blade. "From a mean fight with my sister," Sylvia said. Lynne smoothed some ointment from one of their prescriptions on Sylvia's skin. The white cream became translucent before dissolving into her glistening red-brown back. Then the white gauze and tape symmetrically applied.

Sylvia shrugged her blouse down. "I didn't know if you'd mind touching me or not." Arch smile.

"Oh Sylvia, of course not." But somehow the sense of rising to the occasion was wrong too. "I'll look at it again in a few days."

Time started sliding by. Nancy Winters often came over from next door to join them for a cup of coffee, and twice she assured Sylvia that some of her best friends were black. Lynne and Sylvia laughed about it when she left. They were in it together.

Soon Lynne returned to her weaving in the early afternoons when Jimmy napped upstairs and Sylvia took David and Susie to the park. She began reading again and if, occasionally, she laid her book aside in helpless anger at the inequality in her and Sylvia's lives, she inevitably finished every book she started.

Sylvia loved the children and they adored her, arguing about who was going to sit next to her at dinner, and taking turns helping her wash her soft cap of short black hair. She wore her wig only when guests were expected.

Each night as Lynne and Sylvia were putting the children to bed Sylvia told them a story. Sometimes the stories began with the closing and opening of the bathtub drain, and other times she said that due to circumstances beyond her imagination the story would be continued the following night. They always gave their father a capsule summary of the evening's tale. Molly the mouse. Junebug and the case of the missing month. Allie the slippery eel.

Lynne bought a large notebook and suggested Sylvia write down the stories. The first was seven hundred and fifty-three words, Sylvia counted them, with no capital letters and one period at the end. Together they worked on how sentences sound.

"Do you hear it, Sylvia? How my voice drops where a period belongs?"

"It's like music," Sylvia said.

Then Sylvia told her about the diary. She pulled out a gray folder with her name on the front. The pages were limp and uneven, all in pencil. Lynne weighed it in her hands, "That's a lot of writing."

Sylvia fanned the pages. "Yeah. Maybe you can read it sometime." Then she put it away again, on the top shelf of the closet, out of the children's reach.

Daily Sylvia talked to friends on the South Side. She called them from the breakfast room while she was setting the table and Lynne was fixing dinner. Her musical voice drifted in and out of different sounds as if controlled by organ stops. A different language for another place. Sylvia had been there two months when the music stopped.

"Shit." The telephone clanged down.

"What's wrong?" Lynne turned around from the stove. Nancy, who had just walked in, raised her eyebrows.

Sylvia slumped into a chair shaking her head. "Allie said word is around I'm going to get smoked if I go back home."

"Smoked?" Nancy repeated, but Lynne knew.

"Shot up." Sylvia wet her lips. "Not dead shot, just enough so it breaks you up a little, or leaves a scar, cripples you maybe."

"But what for, Sylvia?" Lynne took her sauce off the stove and turned down the heat.

"Can't you go to the police?" Nancy asked.

"The po-lice! They're the ones caused the whole thing. You people don't understand about police." She sighed. "Mama always said I'm at the wrong place at the wrong time. Last fall I seen something I wished I hadn't seen and those no-good gals with me ratted to the pigs and then said I told. And now Trainer's in jail and his friends are out looking for me. I gotta get it fixed or I can't go home. I gotta call Willy. He'll make it right." She left to get her red book of telephone numbers.

Nancy shook her head. "Christ, that's all we need. The Young Vice Lords, or whatever they call themselves, marching on Winnetka."

Willy wasn't home. "You tell him call me tonight, that it's important. And don't be giving this number out till you see him, you hear?" She had taken off her wig and was running a hand over her hair.

"What can Willy do?"

"Willy's the High Priest of the Scorpions. The ones I told you about. He's big and mean and if he tells Trainer's friends it wasn't me I'll be OK. I was up here anyway so how could I have ratted on him." Logic lulled her features smooth. "But Sharker sure better find Willy tonight."

That evening Sylvia went around with Lynne to check the children and put out lights as George locked up. Lynne heard her recheck the back door five minutes later. The phone rang at two o'clock. George answered. "It's for Sylvia, for God's sake. Hell of a time to call."

When Sylvia didn't respond to Lynne's knocking, Lynne opened the door and gently pushed at her shoulder.

"Sylvia," she called softly.

The sheet flew back from her long arms and Sylvia cringed against the wall, eyes wide.

"Sylvia, it's only me. There's a phone call for you."

Lynne waited in the dark kitchen till Sylvia finished talking. They met at the steps.

"That was Willy. He's seeing Trainer's friends tomorrow to clear it up."

Lynne nodded.

"He's calling back tomorrow after he sees them. Then he's going to get them gals who did the lying."

"Well, you'll sleep better now," Lynne said. And for her, later, the justice was done in an alley she couldn't remember ever seeing, against a brick wall where two girls stood, faceless, and then she smelled something burning and felt like she couldn't breathe till George woke her saying, "Lynne, Lynne. You must be dreaming."

Two days later Sylvia said Willy had taken care of everything.

April 17 1972 it's called the audy home and I been rotting in solitary for three days and I can tell from the start I ain't going to like this place cause when I saw the other gals at supper for the first time I knew being tough is the only thing that's going to keep me alive since everything I've heard about this place looks to be as true as my mama says it was and the smell and the roaches are getting into my clothes and at supper I got a look on my face that said don't fuck with me baby and after the queen tried to take my break and I give her the elbow she let me alone for now but that ain't saying it ain't going to get a whole lot worse before it gets better.

Throughout the summer Sylvia worked for five days and went home on weekends. Mornings were spent washing and folding clothes, running the vacuum, Lynne and Sylvia together. Afternoons were interludes at the beach and parks. By the end of July Sylvia announced she had written twenty-three stories.

But it was too hot in Chicago.

A man, first thought to be an animal, was found skinned and cut up in a garbage can two blocks from Sylvia's apartment. Sylvia knew him. "Ben, he was a bad one. I knew he'd get it some day but no one deserves to die that way, like an alley cat that screamed once too many times."

"Dying is sacred," Lynne said and her words were cool with children playing outside in the sand, not hot with heated streets and dying vegetables.

"Mrs. Hollander," Sylvia said. "There's something I want to tell you about."

Lynne stiffened, waiting for that other world to blur the edges of her own. She loved Sylvia here in Winnetka, she hadn't known her in another place. Sunlight warmed the folded clothes on the table between them, just washed and dried. Sylvia unfolded one of David's shirts.

"Do you remember that old woman in Evanston that was killed a year ago?"

Lynne shook her head "no" before the answer came.

"Well that was pinned on me."

"Sylvia!" They looked at each other across the table.

"I was there like Mama says in the wrong place at the wrong time. I didn't do it but I spent time in jail and I sure know I ain't never going back."

And then she remembered the headlines. An elderly woman and her sister in a Volkswagen had pulled to the curb and were told to hand over their purses, which they refused to do, and *the driver was killed*. Then there followed an account of a wild chase down Lake Shore Drive to the South Side until the car ran out of gas and they were caught and Lynne thought "who?" Sylvia? Our Sylvia?

"Oh, Sylvia." She didn't know what to say.

"I was in the car with Skye, he's the one that shot her, there were four of us, three guys and me, and another car with Allie in it but they got away and when they hauled us in them three decided to hang it on me and they almost got me put away but some lawyer knew I didn't do it and he got me off. The woman's sister told them it wasn't me."

"But what happened to the one that did it?"

Sylvia shrugged. "Skye, he got off too. Even after the lady put the finger on him. She knew him. But the lawyers got her confused. That's what happens most of the time. It's why the cops drag us to the lake and work us over instead of taking us in to the station house."

Outside the window, Susie and Jimmy and David were all in the sandbox now, each with his own bucket and shovel and corner. Jimmy was sifting sand for small stones and leaves to be tossed over the side onto the grass.

Sylvia refolded David's shirt. "I had to tell you. I can't sleep with the nightmares and knowing you didn't know, seeing it painted on my eyelids with my head on your pillow and the kids asleep upstairs."

Lynne sighed and smoothed the towels in front of her. There had almost been too much said for her to hold it all.

"I guess I want to know if I can stay." Her brown hands smoothed the white clothes. In the background came the muted cries of children playing in the sun. Sylvia. Here in Winnetka.

"I'm glad you told me. I'm shocked as I guess you can tell." She stopped to control her voice, relax her throat. "But I'll get over it. Of course you can stay. Why should you go?"

Sylvia nodded, still looking down. "I like it here. Quiet. Like a hospital zone in the city. It's different. Like how I even got this job. We were just in that agency watching TV cause it was raining out and Willy's car had a flat tire and the agency man asked if anyone wanted a job for a few weeks. You should see where my sisters and brothers go to school. Even the colors are different. Nothing's green in the city."

"You're here now," Lynne said firmly. But where, really, is that, she had to add to herself.

September 7 1973 today is the start of my second week back home and it sure feels great even if we are three to a bed with an occasional rat bridging us to the table and I was trying to be a good girl and staying away from junebug and allie and all them cats with their drugs and booze cause I promised mama when she came to the home to get me and cried all over her good black dress and said why wasn't I like my older sisters who never got in no more trouble than just having babies which hurt me a lot cause after I was fourteen and raped bad when the doctor said I can't never have babies and that's what I'd love more than anything in the whole world a little tiny baby and then when junebug said they had some special stuff I told mama I was staying after school to help the teacher cover books and took off over to the vacant lot on tenth street where they were waiting for me and allie and they said true cause it was fine grass and the ride smoother and higher than I've ever been and when I got home I said I didn't feel well and went to bed and watched the moon bend the city into stars and then I cried for mama for she didn't know and I couldn't tell her and I loved her and the moon and the stars and only they knew what my night was like.

And so Sylvia stayed. George said, "Christ, I know what the city's like, I'm there every day. Let her stay." Molly the mouse had children

—ten. Junebug discovered a new planet next to Mars which had stolen the missing month. Allie the eel was learning to read. But just when Sylvia seemed to be absorbed into their lives, Lynne could see her soul slowly collect itself together, she could see her begin to long for the hot streets and sidewalk talk, the tense moment in the loose, long stride.

One Saturday morning on their way to the beach, they dropped Sylvia at the train. It was her first visit home in a month and she checked the train schedule every two minutes till she heard it coming down the track. She waved, running away from them, promising to bring back candy for the children. She was wearing Lynne's yellow shirt and she looked good.

Monday the call came. Sylvia's mother.

"Mrs. Hollander? I'm calling from the hospital for Sylvia cause she can't talk. They won't let her talk to you or anyone."

"What happened?" Lynne frantically looked around for a pencil. "Where are you?"

"She ain't hurt bad. She be out in two days but they're taking her to the jail first and I got to post bond and I don't have no money for that when there's another baby on the way needing clothes, and my youngest sickly all the time so Sylvia said to ask you. She talks about you a lot. It ain't her fault. She fainted on the steps outside the apartment and cut her head open and the neighbors got scared when they seen all the blood and called the ambulance and the police come too and heard my Sylvia mumbling about a gun in some drawer that she'd bought me and they went into my rooms and took it and now they won't let her out unless I pay them a hundred dollars bond money. Can you help me, Mrs. Hollander? Sylvia says you'll help, but if you can't that's all right too. I keep telling her to be a good girl."

"When do you need the money and where do we take it? My husband—somebody will bring it down." Lynne shook her head as Sylvia's mother said she'd put the police matron on the phone for the address. Lynne heard a firm "Hello."

"You're..."

"I'm just the matron in charge here."

"What's going to happen?"

"I don't know anything about the case. Call the station if you want to know what happened. She ain't bad off for the fall she took. Her mother's been here all the time."

"You're by her bed now. Tell Sylvia I said. . . tell her I said we'll help her. Not to worry."

"I'll tell her. And like I said, you better call the station."

Lynne wrote the address of the hospital on the top of the morning newspaper. Then she sat there with her head in her hands, not wanting to call — for Sylvia. But needing to know. She washed the breakfast dishes and made the beds before she dialed information. For the station.

"Captain Stonier here."

"Hello. This is Mrs. Hollander. I am calling from Winnetka about a girl who works for me. Sylvia Marsden. She's being held on some charges."

"Lemme get the books. Sylvia Marsden. Sylvia Marsden. Here it is. Booked on Sunday at 3:00 P.M. Suspected of a heavy dose of drugs. Carrying an unregistered firearm. Loaded."

"Carrying the gun?"

"It was in her purse. She's a bad one, we got a long list on her."

"But she's been working for me and has never. . ."

"Lady, *you got to be kidding.*"

"But I know her. . ."

"And I'm telling you: *Get rid of her.* We got enough trouble."

Lynne waited, pacing the kitchen, for George to come home. The children, as if sensing something wrong, played together without fighting. Built forts in the playroom, quietly asked for crackers, juice. Asked when Sylvia was coming back.

He, too, knew immediately when she met him at the door. The toys strewn around the house. The absence of Sylvia's voice. Her own face. Tensely she told him the facts. Both versions. He called the hospital and told Sylvia's mother he'd be at the courthouse Wednesday afternoon with the money. Lynne's throat ached to talk about it. But there wasn't anything to say, yet. Together they put the children into bed. George read them *Goodnight Moon* while she cried quietly in the living room.

On Wednesday George came home an hour earlier than usual. He took off his tie. Loosened his collar. "I got there too late. The judge called her up early and let her out on personal recognizance. She left word with a woman in her cell that she was glad we were willing to help her, that she'd be calling you soon."

His last words had been in the air before he'd said them and she knew that if the call came this moment that her voice would fail her, that what she had to say, offer, do, wasn't anywhere her mind could focus on. Only the questions.

"What do I say?" Lynne asked, holding out her hands as if to cradle some fragile answer. "Should we have her back?"

"Christ, I don't know, Lynne. After today. I just don't know. Down there it's a different world." His voice was tired, empty. "It's up to you. Whatever you decide."

And then, two days later, her call:

"Mrs. Hollander. I'm out."

"Sylvia. How *are* you? Your face."

"Oh, I'm all right. It don't show and the stitches kept it good and tight." A pause. "What are the kids doing?"

"They're out in the yard spreading more sand around." Lynne could see them, each in his own territory, building castles, roads that would never touch.

"I'll bet they got most of it in their hair. I sure miss them."

"They miss you too. We all do. They said my stories aren't as good as yours. Even the books."

"I have to go back to court next month. On a Thursday. But I would work that Monday before, to make up for it."

"What happened when you went home, Sylvia?" Lynne closed her eyes but they were too full already and soon the receiver slid wet against her cheek.

"Didn't Mama tell you? I guess I fainted. The neighbors called the ambulance and I must have been saying wild things about a gun cause they broke into Mama's rooms and found the gun Junebug just give me. And then they booked me."

"What does that mean?" Lynne asked.

"I don't know. Mama said she'd get a lawyer and go to court with me. Even if it goes wrong I'd just get suspended." Sylvia's voice pleaded.

"Sylvia, we've decided not to have anyone helping us out for a while. Maybe in a few months." *And it was done.*

"Mrs. Hollander, you don't think I would have brought that gun back around those children do you?"

"Oh, Sylvia. I know you wouldn't have. It's just that for a while we've decided to manage, not to spend the extra money." She knew Sylvia was crying in the silence.

"I know what you're saying, Mrs. Hollander. It's all right. I understand."

"I'm sorry, Sylvia." A pause. "Let us know what you're doing. We'd love hearing from you."

"Yeah, I'll call you sometime. I will."

"Mr. Hollander will bring your things down in the next few days to save you a trip."

"Say good-bye to the kids for me, will you. Keep some of my stories for them if you can read my writing. And tell them good-bye."

"Yes, I'll tell them. Good-bye, Sylvia. Take care."

The diary was still there. The pages kept blurring as she read. It took her four hours to finish two hundred and some odd pages of penciled script.

February 3 1974 I knew I shouldn't have gone when them two cars pulled up to the curb and allie she yelled for me to come along that they was going for a ride in whitey's town and I had promised mama I wouldn't get in no more trouble but there was this cool dude driving and he was looking at me like he knowed what turns me on and I thought just let him try so I went and got in the car with the driver called spade and he handed me a joint and looked me over again close up real cool and allie was in the other car and we took off and I was thinking that the real fun was coming later when spade's hand on my knee would be higher and round and I'd be laying down instead of sitting up straight as his hand stayed still and gentle and then somehow I was on that wild ride home missing cars and people I thought we'd get killed we was going so fast and then funny-like just a few sputters and we was stopped and skye threw the gun out of the car so they'd know we wouldn't put up a fight and then they took us in them three dudes and me and they put me in the women's part and

*I didn't have no paper for days and then when the matron finally
gave me some the lawyer said I better not go writing anything that
would get me in more trouble so I put my thoughts away and just
concentrated on hating that matron who shaved my head and cut my
food in half everytime she felt like letting me know that I was a nigger
and she wasn't and how I knew that if I could kill anyone it would be
her and wished it had been her that skye shot instead of that lady's
sister cause she was nice for all she was a whitey and it was her that let
them know I didn't do it and all I can hear when I see her is her
screaming when her sister was shot and hanging on the steering wheel
which gave off a big honk that went away leaving her wailing that
wouldn't she just speak once but I could tell even from where I was
hunched up in the back of the car that her sister wasn't ever going to
call no black a dirty nigger ever again.*

They all missed Sylvia, even the summer seemed to follow her
away. Lynne's voice was strong, not gentle, after she put the loom
aside. They were five at table now, their music thinner as if a chord
had changed. Books were put back on the shelf. Unswept sand
crunched underfoot in the kitchen. In the yard weeds seemed to find
their own water from the dry days.

One day in early September Lynne knelt, grooming the flowers,
refereeing the children's play. She pushed her hair back with her arm.
She was thirsty.

Just as she came in from the garden she saw the battered car stop in
the street in front of their house. Three black boys, men, sat talking.
Names rang in her ears: Junebug, Willie, Sharker, Spade, Trainer,
Skye. She was pulling, tearing off her gloves when the doorbell rang.
Susie and David were in the back yard and only Jimmy was in the
house with her. Upstairs. All those steps. From the dining room she
could see him looking in. Which one was it? She crept softly through
the back hall, then up the stairs to the nursery. She was lifting Jimmy
from his crib as the doorbell rang again. Then, holding him tight
against her stomach, his wet diaper soaking through her dress, she
ran back downstairs, through the hall, her hand on Jimmy's mouth.
He was still there. Big, black. She edged through the kitchen and out
the back door. Pushing David, pulling Susie, she dragged them

through the hedge to Nancy's house. She didn't look back as she pushed them in and slammed the door. She leaned against the kitchen table. Jimmy still held on to her dress, crying. Susie started to cry, backing away from her. Through the hallway she saw Nancy closing the front door. "Lock it, lock it," she cried as Nancy stared and then ran toward her. Then David was crying too and she was telling Nancy, "Sylvia's friends. They're at my house. Call George."

Nancy pulled Susie and David to her, saying fiercely, "Christ, Lynne, get hold of yourself. They were just selling magazines." And Lynne didn't hear anymore. *Sylvia. Sylvia.* Her world caught in her throat.

Patterns

He waited for her. Straining against the pillow to hear past the rain, into the hallway, beyond the night. He had seen her only once through a carefully controlled slit in the doorway when the clear separation of sleeping and waiting began. She was an old woman who cleaned something in the city between five and twelve at night, probably an office building, he didn't know where. The whole city of Chicago needed cleaning. She carried clothes there and back—working clothes, clean going dirty coming—and washed them in the morning. But not regularly enough for him to depend on it. Not like her coming home in the night.

At 1:30 A.M. he always waited for her. She was a part of the rhythm of his night. First her hands fumbling at the latch. The crackle of brown bags squeezed against the door to hold them up. The grating of the key pulling back the lock. Then the door opening and sliding shut against her back, against the coat buttons on her belt. Ever since he'd moved into this first-floor apartment his sleep had been broken by her coming home. Finally he'd begun to wait for her before he slept. As he waited now.

He pushed the pillow away from him, against the wall beside the bed and lay there, his ear pressed into the mattress listening for her steps. She was late. After how many months? Seven? After all that time, tonight she was late. It was something he hadn't bargained for.

The rain was too loud, was growing louder. The mattress felt like a damp gray sponge. He'd never hear her coming up the walk. Her brown bags wouldn't crackle against the door. He could almost smell the mustiness of wet brown grocery bags, soggy with rain.

Tonight he'd have to see her return.

He sat up in the dark, pulling the top sheet around his shoulders. His pant legs caught on the mattress as he slid out of bed, stretching his bare feet to the cold tile floor. He checked for cockroaches before standing up. The sheet dragged behind him. Quickly he pulled it back around his shoulders and looped it over his left arm — a silly gesture. He threw the sheet to the floor, then stood on it to warm his feet. The indignities were beginning to overwhelm him and still she didn't come.

He crossed to the window overlooking the front stoop and the four steps leading up to the door. He couldn't see a thing, the night was melting down his window, dripping through the rotten sill to the floor. He was standing in a puddle on the floor. He turned back to the bed to get the sheet and pushed it with his feet to the wet spot under the window, bunching it against the wall to catch the neon of the street before it burned the room.

Again he peered out of the window looking for her, swearing at his blurred vision. He wiped the glass but the sound of steady drizzle grew louder. How would he know when she came in? Even then he probably wouldn't sleep. It didn't seem fair — as soon as he moved to a different place he started to depend on new things — but they always betrayed him in the end.

He returned to the bed and sat with his back against the wall. He'd have to move this time too, learn a new route to work, try out new laundromats, put his stamp on a particular booth in some diner. But later. Now he felt around the room for his jacket and pulled it on. Then he shook his shoes to get the spiders out and squeezed into them, the buckles flapping open as he walked to the door.

How could she have done this to him? He liked going to sleep after she returned. He always pictured her climbing the steps slowly because her feet hurt or her legs ached. Rolling her stockings down like his foster mothers used to do years ago. Then sitting down with a cup of hot milk or steaming tea, swirling teaspoons of sugar into each cup. And never knowing that he waited for her like a guardian angel. But she'd know now, the bitch.

He stood on the porch thinking about being wet because soon he'd be out there in the rain, looking for her through the sheets of gray that came in waves merging city and lake. He hunched his shoulders as if carrying his full mailbag and started up the street toward the station where she rode the train to and from the city. The rain soaked his skin in seconds and he had trouble keeping his eyes open, alert. The hoot of the train came and went.

When he saw her a great sense of calm washed over him as if the rain suddenly had turned several degrees warmer, but he didn't hate her less for ruining his night.

She didn't recognize him when he stumbled toward her. She in fact had never seen him, he remembered. He'd be just another thin young man to her. "You're late," he said, "where were you?"

"Late?" she said, peering at him, puzzled. She wore a transparent rain scarf, the kind that comes folded in small plastic squares. A black umbrella swayed above her. She clutched her bags tighter to her chest. They didn't crackle, he thought. He had known they wouldn't crackle.

"Why were you late?" he asked again, not expecting an answer because she didn't have an excuse which would satisfy him. She tried to edge by, looking at him like he was nothing out of his uniform. Not exactly nothing, because her eyebrows pushed her forehead into wrinkles of fear. She was older than he thought and her face seemed to be breaking into a thousand tiny lines. Because of the rain her bags didn't crackle when they dropped to the sidewalk. They just settled into being there. The umbrella spun away like a top. And because of the rain her neck was slippery and it was harder to do this time, his hands were sliding and her eyes were too close. Finally he pulled her dress collar up and this time his fingers didn't slide as they pressed in. He'd let her know he couldn't wait forever — these people intruding their patterns into his life and setting his time when he didn't want it set.

He squeezed harder and harder and she started to blur and suddenly his arms hurt, ached, and he realized he was holding her up, supporting her weight because her legs had faded beneath her and she no longer breathed.

He draped her next to the soggy brown bags on the sidewalk and went home. Shivering, he took off his wet clothes and folded them over a chair to dry. He balanced his shoes on the radiator and then rummaged around for a clean sheet. He hoped he'd be able to sleep although it was doubtful.

Two days later she was a one-inch news item in the *Tribune*. The next day, after work when he still wore his uniform, he was asked routine questions by a bored, stupid policeman who kept answering the questions for him. "You didn't know the old woman on the next floor, did you?" No, he didn't. "You probably don't have anything to add to what we know about her, do you?" No, he didn't; he didn't mix much. The policeman checked off his name on a list of people from the apartment. He didn't know them either, he said. Living like he did. Keeping to himself.

He didn't move right away, just went to work as usual delivering the mail on Chicago's North Side. On schedule putting letters and bills and circulars in the mailboxes and door slots, walking the rows of houses which seemed more permanent than any tenant inside. It suited him: walking his route day after day, making a pattern in space and time with the color of his blue uniform, the shape of his brown leather bag. Except for the dogs, nipping at his heels, barking up his legs, slowing his pace. And the owner always smiling as if his precocious child had just said a four-letter word. Now he carried a squirt gun filled with ammonia so he moved right along. "Like clockwork," his people said. "We could set our clocks by you," they said beaming at him, pale women in baggy wool dresses who had survived their husbands to live alone on luncheons and cards, or faded men who still subscribed to their thin professional magazines. They depended on him. For the most part he depended on himself. A few exceptions imposed themselves on his life — and he put up with them for a time — as long as they were dependable, but twice something had gone wrong, he'd been betrayed, and then he was forced to break the habit. Now that the old cleaning woman was gone, he went to sleep earlier. But occasionally he'd wake at 1:30 and listen for her step before he caught himself. The third time this happened he decided to move.

He spent the next three weekends viewing apartments but something seemed always to be wrong. Too many people with their nasty habits, too many sounds. He wanted his next home to be permanent, and somehow he felt more strongly about this than he ever had before.

On the fourth weekend he discovered that he and Mrs. Peck wanted the same thing:

> Wanted: Quiet gentleman to rent rooms in my home.
> Separate entrance. Utilities provided. Must have
> recent references.

He presented himself to her on Saturday after he delivered the day's mail. He was still wearing his blue uniform — in fact he'd planned it that way. Mrs. Peck was suitably impressed.

"Karl Hummer, a mailman," she said, stepping back for him to enter her home. "A mailman." The words seemed to please her.

He stepped past her in his uniform as true-blue as the sky, into a dark room which seemed filled with a million tables — round tables, square, oblong, tiered. He stopped and waited for Mrs. Peck to lead the way. His uniform had faded to a dull gray. He wondered if the rooms to rent were also this dark.

"I keep the house closed up so things won't fade," she said, pulling open the curtains of a wide bay window, turning his uniform back to blue. She smiled at him and motioned for him to follow her. He took small steps past dozens of tiny tables covered with knickknacks he didn't recognize. Paths seemed to be set out among the tables in the rooms as though in a forest. She led him through the living room and dining room to the kitchen, which smelled of freshly baked bread. Three golden loaves stood cooling on a wire rack on another table. His stomach seemed suddenly empty. He followed her past the bread into a well-stocked pantry where she turned to him in front of a door to explain that this was the inside entrance which would of course be locked when someone moved into the rooms. He nodded. She was a foot shorter than he. Frail. He could see her scalp through the thin ribbons of hair held in place by a pink net.

The pantry door opened into a large room — the living room, explained Mrs. Peck — which led to another smaller room, the bedroom. The kitchen and bathroom were situated at the back of the living room. "The stove is old but it works fine." Mrs. Peck opened the oven for his inspection. He watched the oven until she closed it. Then they stood in the living room looking around. The light was good. The furnishings were comfortable, not too crowded so as to need paths. His entrance opened out onto a small porch and down two steps to a narrow cement driveway. No car, he said, so he needn't see the garage. But the apartment was perfect. He'd take it.

They returned to Mrs. Peck's living room. He sat on a low lumpy couch behind two coffee tables filled with china figurines and silver-framed pictures of children in old-fashioned dresses. Mrs. Peck sat across the room from him in a wing chair which seemed to absorb her into its flowered pattern. She must be about seventy, he thought, pretty dotty too. And still living alone. Yes, she lived alone, she told him, she liked being independent and having her things where she wanted them instead of stored in boxes in her daughter's attic or her son's basement. Her bright eyes sparkled out at him from behind gold-rimmed glasses. She couldn't have weighed more than seventy pounds. He pictured her floating over the tables. Arranging china plates and knickknacks from the air. Hovering gently. Independently. He was a mailman, he told her again, he led a simple life. Ate out or cooked for himself. Had few friends. No pets. Didn't drink, smoke, swear. That he also didn't fornicate hung in the air between them — was understood. He in his sky-blue suit and she in her wrinkles and ribs. They suited one another. He gave her twenty dollars as a deposit. He would move in next Saturday. She giggled and patted her hair net. When he left she gave him a letter to mail for her. "Imagine, a mailman," she said.

He could imagine anything.

The following week, during the evenings, he packed carefully. How little he had always surprised him. Pleasantly. He packed his stamp books first, putting them in a newspaper-lined box, then pulled them out again to look through. All new and unpretentious. Collected at random. Pasted in with the help of a small plastic T-bar. He liked the colors. The square corners.

A young guy, new at the post office, helped him move. He was a do-gooder from Old Town. Karl wouldn't have to repay him because that's what do-gooders do best — one-way good deeds.

A curtain moved in the bay window as their pickup truck pulled past Mrs. Peck's front door to his rear entrance. She came floating around the corner of the house as they opened the trunk of the car. "Here's your key," she said, glowing at the two blue uniforms in her driveway. Karl thanked her. She stood there until they went to the door and then slowly followed as if to watch them opening a gift. The rooms sparkled. A fresh loaf of bread announced itself in the kitchen. Lysol in the bathroom. "I thought I'd freshen it up a bit," she twittered from the doorway.

Karl nodded his thanks.

Mrs. Peck started toward the door leading into her pantry then changed her mind and left by his "private" entrance. "Just make yourself at home," she called. "And remember to change your address at the post office."

By the end of the first week he had established himself in his new quarters and decided a number of things. He knew the way he would go to work every day. Two blocks right, two blocks left, then he'd catch an Addison bus going east. He'd ride past the skeleton of the old River View amusement park, annoyed by its bleakness, surprised that nothing had taken its place. He'd change buses at the stadium at Clark Street and continue on south to Belmont. Then off and a few more blocks to the post office. There, his past routine caught up with the present. He went home the same way, backwards. On Saturdays he did his grocery shopping at a store three blocks from his new home. The list was always the same. Except that after three weeks the bread was beginning to pile up on him.

At first he hadn't noticed. But three Saturdays later when he was putting the third loaf on top of the refrigerator he realized he needn't have bought more bread. Mrs. Peck had stopped by every now and then with a fresh loaf, saying it was no trouble at all to bake an extra — she knew how much men liked fresh bread. He enjoyed the sound of her last sentence. He had accepted it graciously and offered to post her mail for her. She would knock on the door between them, lightly. He pictured her with her pink net against the door listening. He imagined hearing her glass frames scraping gently as she inclined her head.

Several times he had the feeling that she waited for him, watched for him to come home in the evening. The curtains seemed to breathe as he passed the windows bordering on the drive. The whole house expanded in a sigh as he entered his rooms. He never heard her moving around in her kitchen on the other side of the wall. The water ran in her sink, the dishes clinked together, but he never heard her step — so he stopped listening for it. He never depended on her own ritual of dinner. She on one side of the wall and he on the other. Sometimes she seemed not to be there. Or had too few dishes to wash. He didn't notice any pattern. The house slept when he left in the morning, swinging his empty leather bag.

A week later Mrs. Peck knocked briskly on the door between them. Karl pushed a saucepan of canned stew off the burner and hurried to open it. Two loaves of bread, one partially eaten and wrapped in saran wrap sat on top of the refrigerator.

This time it was soup. Homemade chicken noodle soup. With thick noodles. "I do hope you don't mind," Mrs. Peck said, behind the steam of the broth like seawind fog. "Sometimes I have too much, the recipes are difficult to reduce." He took the hot soup from her and put it on the table. It glistened under the lamplight. He thanked her. And no, she wouldn't stay. Just hoped he enjoyed the soup.

After she left he sat at the table for a while looking at the soup as if it held some mystery. Then he ate it. Later, cleaning up, he put the leftover stew in the saucepan, covered it, and placed it in the fridge for tomorrow. He returned Mrs. Peck's dish on his way to work the next morning. She gave him two letters to mail.

A month later the stew was still on a shelf below the milk. When it began to smell he threw it out, scraping the sides of the bowl where a green mold had grown. He had a sense of something else growing too.

Minutes later he heard a soft tapping on the tissue between their rooms; the wall almost seemed transparent now. He opened the door and wordlessly, but smiling, Mrs. Peck stepped through.

"Just a little tuna casserole," she said, holding the steaming dish before her. She never lingered, so tonight he held up his hand, asking her to wait. He saw fear in her eyes mirroring the fear in his. "I hope you don't mind, Mr. Hummer," she said, tilting her head.

"Not at all. In fact, I've come to depend on you." He nodded as he saw her surprise. "I'll pay you more per month for supper, but you must be dependable."

She raised her chin to him as though sniffing the casserole she held in her hands between them. "I am honored, Mr. Hummer."

He took the dish from her and set it on the table. "Thank you, Mrs. Peck."

Her chin still high, she continued, "I usually happen to see you when you pass the front windows after work. Your dinner will be ready an hour from that time." Then she turned and closed the door after her, firmly erasing it forever from their mind.

A Man of His Time

Stan Dector knew when the final good-bye had been said. Something was always missing. This time it was the rubber tree.

Marna, his latest roommate, had hauled off the six-foot rubber plant that had flourished in the bay window overlooking Lake Michigan since she had moved in last year. It could not have been a graceful exit and must have required the help of a new boyfriend or a moving company.

Her clothes were gone too, of course, but clothes had come and gone before without the tolling of the final bell. Stan knew from experience that suitcases are too easily packed — and unpacked — and he always waited in suspense until his current girl friend either returned to unpack in remorse or arrived to remove an object she had missed in her flight. Marna had taken both her clothes *and* the rubber tree. It was good-bye.

He missed Marna, for a few weeks. He had loved her in the beginning, in his way. He always loved them. It was a point of honor with him. But, as happens, he had lost the passion of the first month, the first year, and by the time they left, the relationships usually resembled the soft flabby marriages of his friends.

He did, however, persist in missing the rubber tree, so he soon bought another and stood it, as before, in the bay window — foreground for his view of the lake below. Marna was more difficult to replace.

During the next month he waited his self-appointed time of mourning, letting news of his freedom drift around the coffee machines at the office and over the telephones of friends. "He's a bachelor again: actually living by himself." He wasn't sure how gossip phrased it but he knew these things were being said. He counted on it.

The following month, he was ready for a woman's touch. However, various dates with women from the office and nearby bars never seemed to lead in the desired direction without the correct set of props. He began making plans. They had always succeeded in the past.

First, he called a respectable appraiser to come and buy his more salable pieces of furniture; the Salvation Army fell heir to the rest. He kept a double bed, a dresser, and a bean-bag chair. The TV and stereo were built in. Marna's taste had been too modern to suit him — all corners and gleams and hard surfaces.

At last when the stage was bare he began planning a cocktail party for one hundred friends and acquaintances; "Your friends welcome too," the invitations read. His reputation for being suave and eccentric (something he had overheard at his last party a year ago) would draw the crowd. After that it was up to him.

He cleared the dining-room bookshelves of the mysteries he loved to read and sent the custodian to his storage area for the box labeled cookbooks. He stuck in a few bookmarks, dog-eared a few pages and carefully arranged them in a haphazard way. Seventeen in all. The largest was the *Larousse,* the smallest a gem on Cantonese, or so he had been told by Kate six years ago. (She had taken all the quiche and souffle dishes, and even the wok, when she left.)

Next he dusted off his large collection of records, everything from jazz to baroque operas, and memorized a few obscure titles. A stop at Kroch's sent him home with *Sexual Politics, The Rebirth of Feminism, The Photographs of Diane Arbus,* two months of *Ms.* magazine, and, from the used-book section, a rather strange-looking book called *Women and Madness.* When a salesclerk pointed out that he was "just scratching the surface" of the women's movement it was exactly what he wanted to hear. He placed these books next to his old copy of *The Feminine Mystique,* which had already been through three parties.

Then he bought strings for his guitar and sat it conspicuously in a corner. He polished his recorder and practiced for a week until he could run a scale without squeaking or losing an octave. He shined his tennis trophies, later to be filled with nuts. His racquets hung on the wall of the bedroom where the coats would be taken. Finally he checked the remaining bookshelves. He'd lost a good prospect once because of some hard-core porno nestled between Aristotle and Marcuse, neither of whom was powerful enough to redeem him in her eyes.

At the last minute he joined a health club and lost fourteen pounds, allowing him to stand legs spread wide with just the slightest hint of a pelvic thrust while talking about the future of modern dance as adopted by ballet.

No time for a beard — just barely enough for a mustache.

The bartenders were hired and told to mix stiff drinks. The bay window was prepared for a small band. The caterers were pseudo-French, expensive and good. A day before the party he bought a new denim sport coat and rented a docile golden retriever named Lady Jane. By party time, Lady Jane came when called.

An hour after the party began the doorman had counted one hundred and sixty-three people. Half a bottle of bourbon later the doorman announced two bears and Stan surmised that two women had arrived in mink.

The noise level assured him the party was a success. Drink in hand, he drifted from group to group, greeting friends and welcoming new faces. Especially attractive women. The music seemed to carry him with an extra bounce, adding a touch of the old Elvis to his saunter. After two drinks he switched to straight tonic water so as not to impair his judgment.

And the women. He had forgotten how beautiful women can be when dressed in something other than a shift or jeans. They glistened louder than their laughter, they illuminated the rooms in which they walked. He wanted one.

And so he must begin. But where? With the black wool and big boobs, or the long blonde hair and freckles? Or the one with the frizzy hair and red, red lips talking about ERA? Or the one standing near the band and moving lightly to its rhythm, swaying a magnificent ass? Or the one leaning on the bookshelf whose eyes seemed to glow the color of charcoal? Yes, he would start with her. With Jane who smiled as she mentioned her name. For her he held *Sexual Politics.* After five minutes he wrote her name and number in the cover. It amused them both.

"I think music loosens people, lets their souls shine through," he said to Curry. Her ass still shifted gently. She agreed with him. They danced for a few minutes — soulmates — and smiled in understanding of the future.

Judith admired the tiny crab crepes while he admired her décolletage; he said he really preferred them with mornay sauce, which takes only minutes to make but was impractical for the party. He led her to his cookbooks and stroked her upper arm as if admiring an elegant bearnaise.

The music and laughter grew louder as liquor floated through the rooms. Stan quickened his pace. Two women listened to the glow of the A-scale sing the distance from his recorder to their gold-pierced ears. They nodded their understanding that *now* was not the time for more.

Sylvia mentioned the tennis racquets. He demonstrated the slice serve that had made him almost unbeatable in class-B tennis, and talked about the myth of the metal racquet to a group that actually included two men. Sylvia had court time at Mid-town Tennis. He challenged her to — a match.

Women flocked to his books. Again, he held *Sexual Politics* and murmured, "I do understand" while glancing around at the poor dunce who'd been invited as a foil and was performing admirably — swilling martinis and reaching down a girl's dress.

In all, he held *Sexual Politics* four times, tapped Betty Friedan twice in a safe place, as if they were old friends, and flipped knowingly through *Ms.* He couldn't bring himself to stroke *Women and Madness,* he found the jacket photo of Phyllis Chesler too unappealing. *Diane Arbus,* unfortunately, had been mislaid after his first demonstration of affection. His walls of art spoke for themselves. Thank God.

Seven ostensibly unattached women declared how they adored decorating. Of these, three were perceptive enough to add, "How empty the apartment will be when we all leave." Mimi offered to stay but he gently turned her down, hinting at future bean-bag orgies. Her willingness and wit, however, were duly appreciated and fully noted for later reference.

Finally, at three in the morning, the last guest left. The good-byes hung in the smoke-filled room like Calder mobiles. Glasses stood abandoned on the floor against the walls. At least forty cigarette butts had been put out in the soil around the new rubber plant. Stan retreated to the bedroom and collapsed while Lady Jane ate what was left of the French hors d'oeuvres.

When everything was tallied up and assessments made, he found that his guests had consumed thirty-seven bottles of booze, four rolls of toilet paper, and seven hundred and fifty dollars' worth of finger food. And he had the names and numbers of eighteen women ranging in age from twenty-three to forty-one. All in move-in condition. And most important, all liberated enough to do it without a license. Sisters every one.

Stage two began. At the top of the list was Jane from the inside cover of *Sexual Politics*. And Stan knew what he wanted. Beautiful, intelligent to a degree (just below his MBA), and a good body were taken for granted. What he searched for beyond these attributes was a girl liberated enough to share expenses and at the same time, domestic enough to keep house for "her man."

In three months he had narrowed the group down to five. In another two weeks it was between two. The next week he went away on vacation before he collapsed from exhaustion. The time had come to choose.

Curry moved in a week later—her clothes, her easel, her paints and brushes. She was a tall brunette with long straight hair and a full, soft figure. And he loved her.

They listened to his records and made love on a blanket in the bay window beneath the rubber plant. They fed each other grapes. She sketched dozens of pictures of him *au naturel*. "Just make it go away," she'd say, "I'm not finished with the picture yet." Squinting scrutiny withers anything. He strummed his guitar and sang to her as she worked behind her easel. With relief Stan relaxed and waited for Curry to wait on him. They waited together.

By the end of two months Stan was puzzled. The apartment

bloomed with their passion and the graphics that Curry sold at out-
rageous prices to the Bröner Gallery, but she showed no inclination
to buy any couches or chairs or rugs — even when he assured her that
he would pay for half. "You can have the bean-bag chair," she said
from her cross-legged position on the floor, "I haven't time for shopping." He finally bought an oriental rug and two wing chairs, which
Curry admired with enthusiasm as she produced a check for half
their cost. *He* did all the cooking when they didn't eat out. "Oh I love
French food," she said, "but I don't like to cook and since you do. . ."
When he didn't cook she ate grapes. With or without passion. She
liked grapes. *He* read the books. "You read them all and tell me what
they say," she said, "I don't need them, I *am* free." And in a sense this
was true. She hadn't really cost him anything and their passion was
blooming larger than ever. Still he had the sense of something having
changed.

A week later, on his way home from the grocery store, he stopped
by the rental agency and asked if he might purchase Lady Jane. "For
a price," the clerk told him, "a high price because she is a particularly
well-trained dog." Stan said he would think it over and hurried home
so the frozen foods wouldn't melt. Curry remembered Lady Jane
from the party and immediately offered to share the cost of *her.* The
next day, Stan bought her a sumptuous basket, which they placed
beneath the rubber tree, and that evening he brought her home. They
agreed that Curry would walk her in the morning and brush her, and
he would feed her and walk her at night. Lady Jane continued to
come when called. And a year later, five years, Stan was only mildly
surprised that he loved Curry more.

Winter Evenings: Spring Night

Sarn woke to muffled sounds of voices in the kitchen. He pushed the covers back and sat up before he realized they were not accompanied by the sounds of morning — water splashing, bacon and eggs crackling in the skillet, roosters crowing, crooning in the chicken yard. Then he noticed the thin yellow light framing three sides of the wooden door leading into the kitchen. So it was night still. He pressed his pillow flat and lay back down to listen. But he didn't hear the soft voice of his mother asking, controlling, and shaping the long silences which were his father. He sat up again and cupped his heels tightly in his hands. It was his father talking.

"But you been taking him with you the last few times out."

Sarn had long since sensed that for his father speech was a form of desperation.

"He ain't going tonight. He's been looking peaked today and feels warm. I put him to bed early." Sarn remembered, smelled warm hands rubbing his chest and back with mustard and water. He breathed deeply as his mother continued, "He won't bother your poker game none. Never did before, did he?"

And again where there would have been silence he heard his father's voice. "It might make him feel better to go." Sarn knew it was the last time his father would speak, he had already outdone himself twice. And then his mother's voice:

"That makes no sense. I don't want him giving anything to Willa Kay's baby." And Sarn was right because only silence followed. He turned over to stare out the window and listen for David's horn. He pictured his mother putting fresh bread and a jar of soup or jam in a brown bag to take along to Willa Kay's. Every Friday night his mother went to the next town over to visit his sister, who'd had a baby girl that winter. Each Friday night his father and five other men played poker at the round oak table in the kitchen next to Sarn's bedroom. All fall and most of winter Sarn had lain in bed and listened to the rise and fall of bids and coins. Only recently had Ma allowed him to go along to Willa Kay's and sleep on the folded blankets beside the couch. He liked Kay and her gentle husband David. And he liked waking in their apartment over Eckert's drugstore to watch the town begin to stretch and move.

Minutes later David's horn blared in the driveway outside his window and the kitchen door opened. "Check on him before you turn in and make sure he's covered," his mother said. "I'll be back tomorrow about noon."

The door closed and David's horn tooted lightly twice down the drive. Sarn shivered and lay back down, pulling the thin patched quilt under his chin. A chair scraped and his father opened the icebox and then a bottle of beer. Sarn wished he were on his way to Kay's, warm and safe between David and his mother in the blue Dodge with the fuzzy dice hanging from the rearview mirror. Instead he lay there wanting another blanket and waiting. Soon he heard footsteps coming toward his door and he turned his head to watch the white knob turning, slowly moving in. Moonlight softened his father's face as he squinted into the darkness, then moved across the squeaking floorboards to the window. Sarn eased up on one elbow, bunching the pillow under him.

His father swung around and motioned to him, "You awake?" The smell of beer was fresh and sharp. "You're all right, huh?"

Sarn nodded. He didn't feel cold anymore but he wasn't warm.

His father took a long drink of beer. "I have something I have to do tonight." He looked back out the window. "I'll have to take you along."

Sarn pushed the covers from him and slipped to the edge of the bed, surprised. "I can come?"

"Yeah, get dressed. Something warm." He rubbed his hand along the bottom of the bed rail. "And no talking about it afterward." He stood there as Sarn dressed, taking a long drink of beer and looking out the window into the spring night. Together they went into the warm kitchen. Sarn could feel his father waiting and watching and he, too, waited and watched.

It was the first snow of winter and Sarn pictured it silently falling, covering the farm in white blankets. The thick frost on the window across from his bed hid most of the night, but he knew night was for listening not for seeing. And tonight they came in as usual, one by one, stamping their feet, rubbing their hands. Cross and Willie from the same mysterious mill as his father, Son Paden from a construction job more off than on. Lefty from the town butcher shop where once a week he cut and carved their evening meals, and finally Hersh came up from the dairy farm down the way. Sarn pulled the quilt closer around him and listened. Chairs scraped across cracked linoleum and beer bottles were opened with soft pops like balloons bursting. Cards were shuffled and the business of the evening began. In turn Sarn gave each voice a name:

Cross: You gonna raise me, Hersh, or you gonna pass?

Hersh: I pass. Goddamn, I sure would like to see them there cards though. (Sounds of candy paper rattling, the smell of warm chocolate.)

Cross: Deal 'em that way again, Joe. (His father dealing.)

Lefty: It's colder than a witch's tit. Can't we get a little more heat in here?

Willie: Jenkinstown hill, it ain't been ashed but once tonight, and George said he didn't know if he'd be able to do it again if the snow keeps up.

Paden: Radio said it's supposed to snow eight more inches. Only a fool'd be out on a night like this, or Danny Parkins knocking off a piece.

Hersh: I hear he's been seeing Tommy Vinton's wife.

Paden: I wouldn't mind none seeing her myself.

Willie: You gonna play, Paden?

The waiting didn't last long as the first car wound up the driveway, bumping over potholes. Sarn's father threw his empty beer bottle into a brown bag under the sink. The car stopped and soon Hersh stepped through the door and looked around. "Guess I'm the first one here," he said. Sarn's father nodded and motioned to a chair, but not to the poker table. Sarn watched as Hersh lifted the chair one-handed over to the stove and straddled it. Then Hersh reached into the pocket of his jacket, brought out a chocolate bar, and carefully unwrapped it. He took a bite and licked his fingers, transferring the bar from one warm hand to another. Then he glanced at Sarn watching him and his jaw missed a step in the parade of thought as he patted his pocket and pulled out another candy bar, also chocolate. Sarn took a couple of steps toward him. Hersh's jaw resumed its rhythm as he unwrapped the second candy bar and with only the slightest hesitation gave Sarn the one he had just been eating.

Now two more cars were grinding, bumping up the hard dirt driveway and Sarn moved over by his father as Hersh scraped his chair around to face the noise. Willie Candlass and Cross came through the door first followed by Son Paden and Lefty Halloran. Son Paden looked around and rubbed his hands together. "Looks like we're all here and ready to go."

Willie laughed, "Me, I'm going to have a beer first. Anyone else?" He crossed to the icebox and Lefty followed, reaching past him for a bottle. Cross zipped up his jacket. "Well, hurry up, we ain't got all night. I'd still like to win back a little of the money I lost last week." They all watched Willie and Lefty drinking their beers. Sarn knew not to move but just stand there, licking his fingers like Hersh did. His tongue felt the candy more than tasted it tonight. "OK. Let's go." Willie tossed his bottle under the sink and settled a red hunting cap on his head. Sarn pulled his jacket on and followed his father. Cross spoke next, sputtering, "Hey, Joe. What the hell you doing? He ain't coming, is he?" Like dominoes the men turned toward his father.

"I ain't got any choice. Jessie left him here. She says he's sick." His father had stopped by the door and turned, brushing Sarn's forehead with his elbow.

Lefty threw his bottle under the sink with a crash and wiped his mouth with the back of his hand. "Hell, I don't much like it." They waited.

"Well, you might as well call it off. There ain't no one driving that there truck but me." Sarn stepped closer to his father. Cross sagged into a chair and Hersh pulled out another chocolate bar. Then his father said, "I can leave him in the truck. He's only six and don't talk much anyway."

"Just like his old man," Son Paden said with a soft punch to Sarn's left arm.

Lefty hitched his thumbs in his belt showing a flash of knife in the heavy leather of the sheath. He said, "Still water runs deep, they say. Old Joe here might have something to tell." Sarn's father swung around to face him.

"Christ," Willie said, pushing Lefty toward the door. "Let's go, we ain't got all night."

They trailed out into the frosty evening. The ground was hard and silent under their feet. Three cars were parked off to the side of the house. Sarn trailed his father to the barn to get the truck. Then they drove back to where the men stood together like a mound of coal against the sky. Cross climbed in the front on the other side of Sarn and the rest swung up on the back. "You got everything, Willie?" Cross called out the window.

Willie thumped the window with his knuckles, "Yeah, let's get rolling."

Snow had been falling steadily although intermittently for a month now and it almost reached up to Sarn's window from drifts made by the wind. And again they came and rubbed their hands and stamped their feet.

Cross: You gonna need some cards, Hersh?

Hersh: Yeah, gimme two.

Willie: Three.

Paden: I know when to get out.

Joe: One.

Cross: You've had more pairs tonight than I've ever seen. Willie?

Willie: I'm out.

Paden: So old Lefty went and got himself married. I knew he was seeing Tootie Sheer but I didn't know it was serious. She's kind of been around, ain't she?

Cross: I'll go for two. Yeah, they went up to Niagara Falls for a few
          days. Seems a little cold for going there this time of year.
Hersh: I'm out.
Willie: I'm out.
Joe: Two and raise you two.
Cross: Hell.
Paden: Never too cold for getting a little. Saw Tommy Vinton's wife
          and Danny Parkins taking off tonight up toward the water
          works.
Willie: You gonna deal, Hersh?

Sarn's father brought the truck to a slow stop about twenty yards
away from a gray frame house with a red door and white ruffled curtains in the lighted windows. A screen door was swinging in the
breeze as though someone were gently rocking it. Moths buzzed and
floated around the porch light. Willie and Son Paden hopped down
from the back of the truck and came around to stand by his father's
window. Willie held a loop of clothesline in one hand. Cross leaned
over Sarn to talk. "You sure he's in there?" Paden snorted and waved
his hand. "Yeah, he's in there. Tommy's been working overtime every
Friday night. Don't get home till after ten." Cross leaned back and
sighed, "It sure is a wonder he ain't been caught before this."

"Get ready, boys," Willie called back to Hersh and Lefty. "He's
coming out."

The red door opened and a man in a bright blue jacket came out.
He turned to the woman who appeared in the doorway behind him
and patted her on the hip. She laughed a slow lazy laugh and Sarn
smiled with her. She was standing there kind of strange, leaning
against the door frame while her left hand smoothed her blouse from
hip to breast and back again as if to prolong some memory.

When she had closed the door, shooing out a moth, Sarn realized
he had almost missed what happened next: Danny came to within ten
feet of the truck before a crooked smile appeared on his face and he
said, "Hi, Willie," and Willie said, "Hi, Danny, you having some fun
tonight?" And Danny said, "Hell it ain't much." And Willie said,
"The hell it ain't." And Hersh and Lefty and Paden grabbed Danny

while Willie tied his hands behind his back and put a white piece of cloth in his mouth and then tied his feet together too so he couldn't walk and had to be carried like a sack of flour to the back of the truck and heaved in. Sarn's father and Cross never moved. Cross finally looked behind him into the truck bed. "I hope they don't get too rough." Willie banged on the window, "OK, we're all in." Sarn's father started the truck and glided out onto the road past the fire hall, then onto the dirt road and up past the Stewert's farm, up toward the old strip mine, a black landscape against the gray sky. "Sure looks deserted enough," Cross said. "He'll have a long walk back." He glanced at Sarn and didn't say any more. Black mounds of coal and weeds filled the sky as they drew near.

Sarn could hear them coming in stomping their feet and cursing the cold and the snow. They finally settled down, one less. The cards had been falling for some time when Lefty arrived.
Cross: You gonna leave early too, Lefty?
Lefty: Just deal the cards, Cross. I ain't going anywhere before I get some of your money.
Cross: Listen to him, would ya. How many, Willie?
Willie: Gimme two.
Paden: One. You sure are in a good mood tonight, Lefty.
Lefty: Three. Christ. I should've stayed home the way the cards are falling.
Willie: I'm out. How's your wife like staying home these days, Lefty?
Lefty: She likes it fine, why?
Willie: I know she likes it fine. I asked if she likes staying home too?
Lefty: Two and up two. And up yours, Candlass. It ain't like no one never had no taste of your wife. Seems to me Danny Parkins used to have her on his list.
Willie: Hell, I put a stop to that, not that it's any business of yours.
Hersh: Four to call.
Willie: Unless Danny's getting tired of Vinton's wife and's looking around for something new.
Lefty: You just better shut the fuck up. I don't have no worries about Tootie, see. None.
Paden: You see 'em as I lay 'em.

Hersh: Christ, a full house.
Lefty: And I better never have, see.
Willie: OK, OK.
Paden: You have to admit old Parkins really gets around.

Sarn's father steered the truck off the old mine road and they bumped along about twenty feet over black weeds before coming to a stop. Cross opened his door and jumped down and then glanced back at Sarn before going around to the back of the truck. Sarn's father pocketed the keys and nudged him with his elbow, "You stay here." Sarn nodded, looking ahead at the black night trying to remember the woman in the red door. The windows were still open and the cool night air drifted in. Sarn moved into his father's place under the steering wheel and then his growing fear made him turn in time to see the men lifting, dragging a bundle of blue jacket out of the truck by the light from an old miner's lamp. Danny's eyes were wide and staring and seemed to be giving directions as he followed the flow of speech from one man to another. And then they started walking and Danny seemed to be walking too and Sarn heard him saying, "Christ, can't you guys give me a break and I'll lay off," and Willie next, "You done enough laying to last you a lifetime," and then they were out of sight except for the jagged light of the lamp but Sarn could still hear over the mounds of coal and dirt Danny pleading, "So help me God I'm telling ya I'm done for good and all with women cause they ain't to a one of them any good anyway," and then he was answered by a chorus of voices and then a stronger voice, Lefty, who said, "How can we be sure?" and then the thudding began and Sarn covered his ears but couldn't shut out the sound of one high piercing scream that made him gasp for day.

They came late that night cause there'd been a fire over the hill and a couple of men had pitched in and given a hand to putting it out. Sarn had been able to see the smoke from his bedroom window as if the old mines were operating again. He listened for details.
Cross: That's one of the biggest fires we've had around here.
Hersh: Yeah, something like that could wreck our plans.

Cross: Come on, deal, Paden.

Willie: You ain't talked about them none have you, Hersh?

Hersh: I said I wouldn't. Why's it such a big thing anyway?

Willie: It ain't. We was just trying to keep it a secret, surprise him. I'll take two.

Paden: We'll meet here as usual.

Lefty: He'll be limping around for a while. I'll bet a hell of a lot of guys would like to get in a few kicks.

Cross: Maybe I better not come being as we're cousins and all.

Willie: Nobody'd suspect you of beating up on your own kin, and he'll be too damned embarrassed to tell.

Cross: I don't know. Lemme think about it.

Paden: Sing it out. Boys, Lefty, how many you want?

Lefty: Three and make 'em good.

Hersh: It don't sound like a joke to me no more.

Lefty: It ain't, but he has it coming to him.

The men returned to the truck behind the miner's lamp in a quiet group but Danny wasn't with them and it sounded like Hersh was crying as if he'd dropped all his chocolate bars. Sarn's father pulled himself in and was starting the motor, pumping the gas, even before the men climbed into the truck. He waited for a silence he seemed to expect before shifting into first and swinging out around over the weeds back to the road, heading home. He drove fast and soon they were stopped in the driveway beside the cars to let the men out. He didn't turn off the motor. In back the men jumped off the truck, quiet, catlike. Hersh must have found some candy cause he was quiet now too. Except for Cross they didn't stay for talk or cards. Their car motors started and together they drove away, slowly like a funeral procession, out to the road. Cross didn't move. His father didn't move, just stared straight ahead to the barn. Cross cleared his throat. "Christ, Lefty must be crazy," he looked across at Sarn's father. "I can still see him plain as day, cuttin' . . ." Cross's words were lost as his father gunned the gas hard and shifted into first. Cross opened his door and jumped down. His fingers held on to the low-ered window, and then louder, "I mean, Christ, why did he have to do that to him?" Cross pulled his hand back fast as the truck jerked forward, bumping down the driveway to the barn. Sarn turned to watch him. Cross didn't move, his arms hung limp at his sides. And then Sarn again heard the scream and this time he knew, and it didn't stop and wouldn't quit, and he couldn't hold it and wet himself, and he put his hands between his legs and pressed hard and his hands were wet and it wouldn't stop.

Sarn lay awake shivering into morning. Several times his father came in and stood looking out the window, up toward the old mines. Once he put another blanket on him. Finally, after drinking some strong tea his father brought him, he slept. Voices in the kitchen wakened him just before the bedroom door opened and his mother came in still in her coat. Her rough hand was warm on his forehead, pressing against his cheeks. He felt tears come and kept his eyes closed tight, but she was smoothing covers over him now, patting the quilt around his shoulders and didn't notice. He was glad when she returned to the kitchen. Until he heard her speak.

"He's sicker than he was when I left," she said. "Didn't you pay him no mind, keep him covered?"

"He'll be OK," his father said.

"Oh, he'll be OK," dishes clattered in the sink and his mother's voice grew louder, "but you should've listened to me, looked in on him. Playing cards, boozing with those no-account men." His father didn't answer.

"Why don't you say something? Well?" But Sarn knew that for his father it had all been said as if words had been stripped away like the coal from the hollows and hills which had once been farms. And he too had nothing to say as he kept his father's silence. For now it was enough that they were home.

Suppertime

Eve sets the table, swishing the morning crumbs off the faded oil-cloth. The heavy plates ring into place like rusted bells. Five spoons and forks. Three knives. Salt and pepper. Butter and jam. Milk pitcher. Five plates. Then standing on the edge of the porch she calls down the hill for Danny and Sally. Waves to her cousin, Earl, as he passes up the hill. "Might be over later," he yells, leaning out his truck window. The rich smell of the roast surprises her as she reenters the kitchen. Like when she was young and her mother was cooking. Now, standing over the stove, stirring, mixing, somehow takes the smell away.

His wife's voice wakens Jack. He knows it isn't time yet. He doesn't open his eyes, not till he's ready. He's deserving of a few winks after slaving all day at the mill. The TV drones in the corner of the room. He holds his breath until he hears her like a screech owl call again. Hears the screen door shut because she must have seen them coming up the hill. The kids both look like her before he closes his mind's eye.

Eve pricks a potato with a fork. Done. Then she slices the bread which has cooled since noon, pours three coffees. "Supper's ready," she calls into the darkened hall. Gray light flickers out of the front room. Couch springs sag as her husband rises and the TV squeals off. In the dining room where her father is saving electricity his rocking chair squeaks into action crunching newspapers, seed catalogues. He enters the kitchen squinting into the bright light as if sighting in on a rabbit or bird. Then he settles into his chair, tucking his napkin in his pants below his belly, saying, "Well, what's it tonight, Verda?" Eve hears him use her mother's name. But he's an old man. She lets it pass.

And there is Verda standing there ignoring him, her back to him, front to the stove. Her apron getting warm. Making him wait till the steaming dish is sitting here on the table uncovered. Where's that daughter, Eve?

Her husband arrives with more ceremony. Scuffing his lead-toe boots. Making marks on her floors no doubt. He pats her on the hip as she is dishing out the food. A little too hard and it stings. She ignores her father who focuses on them as if he half-remembers some similar gesture he once used on her mother and then his eyes blur and he reaches for the first dish she sets before him. Tonight it is the mushrooms and peas.

Jack looks at her twice. His wife's face is flushed from the steam or something. Almost pretty like it used to be when they were going together. He gives her another pat on the ass and moves to the table beside his father-in-law — God, the old man smells. The coarse weave of her skirt lingers on his fingers. He cups his hand around his balls, lifts, and settles himself on the hard kitchen chair.

Only his wife Verda is serving tonight. Must be his daughter is off with that fellow again, marching her titties around for everyone to see. No. It is his daughter serving. He peeks around to his left and sees that fellow, Jack, sitting at the table too. Well now.

Panting, Danny and Sally enter the kitchen door. Danny slams it hard and watches as the old man drops some peas in his lap, then tries to put them one by one into his mouth. He watches fascinated when the old man bends his head and a few more fall out. Sally begins to giggle and he gives her a push to show he didn't slam the door on her account. He sets his lunch pail down hard too.

"Stop slamming that door. Think all I got money for is new glass."
Jack pushes his father-in-law's plate a little closer to him. It works.
The old man's fork returns to the plate, spears a piece of meat. And
then his mouth closes over it just in time, just before his top teeth
begin to slide loose and drop. Jack looks away as his stomach turns.
He slices the meat on his own plate into bite-sized pieces. "Sit down."
He points the kids to their chairs with his knife.

Eve feels the tension coming on. Her husband's nostrils are moving in and out, his teeth clenched tight. Her father goes on eating.
Eating through another year. How many more years until they can
sell the farm and move into one of those neat row houses on the outside of town? Only come back here twice a year to tend the graves,
plant flowers. When there's two instead of just her mother's one. She
remembers Earl is coming over. He ain't brought up buying the farm
for a while. But maybe tonight ain't right either.

Finally, as the old man's chewing a piece of meat, he glares at his
grandson sitting on his right. Damn kid got no respect. And his son-
in-law only yelling at the kid, not giving him the licking he deserves.
Lily-livered-son-of-a-bitch had to be dragged back here to make an
honest woman of his daughter and then staying on to clutter up the
house with yet another kid. Pushing his plate around, thinking he
don't notice. He swallows, careful to keep his teeth in place. Then he
shows Jack what he can do with a fork. He stabs a piece of meat
through to his plate. Verda would turn in her grave to see what passes
for a son-in-law lording it over her table now.

Eve hears Earl's truck pull up the gravel of the drive and rises to get
him a plate and silver. Tucks in her hair. He's already eaten but he
likes her cooking. He crosses to the porch and enters. No knocking
with kin he says to her when he comes over in the afternoons. The old
man goes on eating. Jack pushes his chair back a ways and nods.
Jack and Earl were never friends but she knows Jack has other
hopes. He knows that Earl stops by now and then. Second cousins
after all. She sighs, lifting her shoulders. She remembers marching in
parades on the Fourth of July. Sunlight glinting on her silver baton.

The crowds waving banners and balloons. Just her out front. No harm done.

Earl waits for the second invitation before sitting down. Eve sure can cook. He leans back into her when she gives him his plate. His arm against her hip. She moves away, but not too fast. "Hey, Uncle Harry," he says loud to the old man, "that horse I bought at auction is looking better after a month of good feed." Earl sees the old man's eyes focus on him, through him. Too bad. He used to be a good judge of horses. What's that smell?

The old man looks right through him to when he come upon Verda and the hired man rolling in the hay. And there she is, there is Verda giving the hired man a feel right in front of him. Never learn.

Sure Jack knows what brings Earl around besides wanting to buy the farm. He don't care. Her guts have gone soft like the rest of her. Pretty once, twirling her baton high in the air. Twitching her skirts. Playing hard to get when they parked out by the dump, then making it impossible for him to let go. Bringing in her father to settle it. Nagging at him now to cinder the driveway, steady up the chicken coop. After working all day at the mill in the fucking-hot furnace room which ain't no joke. Tying him down to the *idea* of a farm, scrubby hills and back roads going nowhere. The old man like an anchor on dry land: out of his element but too rusted to move. Jack leans forward, rises a little from his chair to reach across for more meat before Earl takes it all. He begins cutting again. It is a sharp knife because he keeps it sharp. Once a week he grinds it, metal on stone. It could almost cut anything. Could even cut him free.

Earl asks Jack about the mill. He put in two years there himself a while ago before coming back to farm. Too dirty, noisy, hot. He tells Danny and Sally to come over Saturday to try out the new horse. Then he says to the old man, "Sure could use some more land seeing as we back up to each other, Uncle Harry. I gotta make decisions pretty soon about maybe moving away to a bigger place if you don't sell to me." He stops.

Jack watches his wife stop her fork in mid-air. Swallow on nothing. She is looking at the old man like someone is pinching her cheeks too hard, pulling on her ears. Maybe remembering the belt she said he used on her till she was sixteen. The old man keeps right on eating like he didn't hear. The bastard. As if he ain't always cleaning his ears with twisted bits of paper. Leaving them around on window sills. Christ, what if Earl moved somewhere else? They'd never get rid of this place. Jack rubs his thumb across the knife blade almost feeling his fingerprints scrape away.

Sally wrinkles her nose and pleads, "Why can't we live in town?" She leans toward her father, her flat chest against the hard edge of the table. "You ain't a farmer like Granpa used to be, or Uncle Earl. And anyways, Uncle Bill and Aunt Lou live in town." She looks sideways at Granpa because somehow in this one question he's the boss. She hates to eat with him. He makes what's in her stomach go the wrong way. She hates being left with him even more, when she has to sit on his lap while he reads her the funnies and squirms. This she don't think about long.

The old man hears but he ain't talking. He feels his anger come around souring his stomach. Damn that Earl, ruining his supper. He wets a little before he squeezes his legs tight to cut it off. And Eve complaining about his wash, his smell. Soaking his overalls so long in lye the odor nearly knocks him over when he puts them on clean. Wanting to sell the farm, and then farming him out — where. Just think about that. Who'd believe she was the same kid who used to play in the barn hay, clean or dirty, while he milked the cows and shoveled feed. Uppity now with her home-ec classes and high school diploma handed out just in time. Was a time these pants had a belt before the suspenders made him sit a little easier, before the cows were sold off and then the chickens, before he needed to sit. There was a time he'd have stood up and whipped his belt out of the loops in one motion. Doubling it over, ready. Verda used to jump right smart.

Earl's words and Pa's silence make Eve jittery. She pours more coffee for the men. She fills Danny's and Sally's plates with the last of the peas. They both make silent faces at her. Then she goes to the stove and refills the blue cracked dish with peas, with mushrooms. Those mushrooms out by the cistern—they almost fooled her at first. Sliced and buttered they'd certainly fool anyone, even the old man. She thinks about it. Thinks about picking a few. Just enough. They are back at the table now, her and the mushrooms and peas. She twists her apron in her lap as the men help themselves to more.

The old man has heard it once too many times. Them whispering together at night, dropping hints when he's eating his supper. "I ain't selling," he says pulling the words out from somewhere deep in his chest. "This land stays together till I'm dead. Then it don't matter. But I ain't saying it again." He stands up, sending his chair flying back against the sink. He pulls his belt out of his pants in one movement. It feels good in his hands. The warmed buckle sinking into his palm.

Earl waits till the steaming coffee is flat on the table before he leans back toward Eve. This time she doesn't pull away. She bends over him and puts her hand on his leg, her breasts are heavy on his shoulder, she smells of sweat and roast beef and fresh bread. And maybe another smell. He covers her hand with his own. Moves it higher on his leg. She comes with the farm.

Christ! The old man must have pissed hisself again, Jack thinks. And he's expected to eat sitting next to a human outhouse. Year after year until they all drown in it. Sinking under the weight of a new roof and furnace for this dump of a house while the barn rots and the pastures grow wild. Till not even Earl will want it, long moved away. Slowly Jack stands and takes his knife. He wipes the particles of meat and gravy off on the edge of the oilcloth. Then he lifts the old man by his suspenders, saying, "You come after me once, but it better not play that way again." He doubles up the gray elastic and slices through it in one pull. The suspenders fall down the old man's back like pigtails. "You and your daughter can sit in this place and rot. I ain't bringing home the dough anymore. You're gonna have to put some potatoes back in the ground to keep eating. Earl can fuck you both. Me, I'm getting out."

Their faces, her father's and Jack's — not the kids' — are turning a little gray. Nervously, Eve begins to talk about canning. Telling them about the tomatoes being too pulpy this year, without much rain, not enough hoeing to bring up the good dirt. Her voice winds down as her father says slowly, "Something don't seem right." He drops his fork and wipes his mouth with the back of his hand. He stares at the table where the food huddles together. Jack edges away from him. Eve can see him hoping it ain't right with the old man. And then Jack begins to stare, but not at the table, at her. The kids stop eating, and watch, whimpering. Earl is standing up with his hands on the back of his chair, his hands are shaking with how close he come. "Oh God," she says, almost remembering the smell of clean warm hay, and the milking, the warmth of the fresh sweet milk.

The old man brings up the other belt-end to form a loop. The kids stand back, eyes wide with the fear he likes to see. Eve cowers in her chair as he pulls Jack up by the collar and throws him against the drainboard. The first swing cuts the bastard somewhere near the same prick that brought Eve home to stay. As Jack doubles over to shield his balls, the old man cuts him hard across the back. The shirt parts as if by magic. And then he pulls Eve from the table, pushes her across the chair. Raises her skirt over her head like he used to when she come home late saying they had a flat tire and him knowing all the while she was sparking at the dump. He raises Verda's skirt like he did when he caught her taking cake to the hired man. "Oh God," she moans. The kids are crying now. Kids? Danny is staring at the red welt rising on his mother's skin and doesn't see him coming. Once is enough for that kid. Sally too. He stands at the window while he threads his belt back through the loops, looking out over the hill toward the fire hall lights. Must be some good poker games tonight. Then he sits down and finishes the potatoes, starts on the rest of the mushrooms and peas.

Jack throws the knife with a whip of his wrist. It pierces the peeling cupboard and stays. Earl moves toward the door. Eve is wailing into her apron. Then Jack climbs the stairs two at a time and stuffs his clothes into an old army bag left over from the only time the old man himself ever got away. Let the old coot support himself and his daughter. He won't come after Jack now. When he gets to Elmer's store at the bottom of the hill he calls Gracie, telling her he's going to give it to her big tonight, not once but twice because once he's there he ain't leaving. What does she think of that?

Jack and Uncle Harry are out of the way somehow. So Earl marries Eve, saving money that way. Maybe they have kids—all boys who stay home, not too bright with big ideas. She asks him every morning what he wants for supper and he tells her. He tells her what he wants after supper too. They get along just fine.

Eve's refrain at the funeral is, "He picked them himself, pottering around Mother's patch. Not kept up like it used to be." Earl asks her to marry but grief makes her reserved. She names a price for the farm. Earl thinks on it a week before deciding to buy. It is too much work for her, being alone with the children and all. So many sad memories. She signs the papers to sell the farm with a shaking hand, and then holds a white lace handkerchief to her nose. A month later she moves to an apartment over Grady's Drugstore and gets a job selling perfume and tobacco while the children are in school. Grief makes her thin like she used to be and she buys bright new clothes. She tries a different perfume each week from samples salesmen leave behind. Her favorite is Evening in Paris. The salesman too.

A fire starts at the stove. A curtain blowing out too far over the flame. They are all dying except Sally who is too speechless to cry warnings. She cries for one month without stopping. She misses her mother and sometimes Danny. She likes her mother's sugar cookies better than Aunt Lou's where she goes to live. Aunt Lou and Uncle Bill have a red brick house near town. She and her friends go to all the movies and to the carnival twice a year. At night she sleeps in a white-ruffled canopy bed. There is a shiny piano in the front room. A doorbell. No other kids. Two cats.

Gas from the stove rises in clouds like a tornado and kills everyone except Danny. He does not cry. He acts like a man and sits and reads. He reads at Uncle Bill's where he goes to live. He misses his mother. Sally not much. He plays baseball after school at the lot near the police station. Makes the team. He has a silly canopy bed. It will soon be replaced with new bunkbeds ordered from the Sears catalogue. There is a bookcase with wavy glass doors in the front room. A brown leather reclining chair. Sidewalks. No other kids. Two cats.

Danny and Sally leave the table just after the apple pie, homework still to do. They carry glasses and plates to the sink and Eve motions them into the dining room to set up their books for the evening. She and her father and Jack and Earl finish up in the silence that settles after the old man announces he don't want no more talk of selling yet. In spite of that they all enjoy a second piece of pie. Needs a little more lemon next time. Then Jack goes back to the TV sending its drone out to the kitchen, where it seems to quiet Eve's nerves tonight. Earl leaves shaking his head. Her father moves to the rocking chair by the window and nods himself to sleep. She cleans off the table. Nibbling on a piece of leftover meat. Finishing up the mushrooms and peas. And then because there is nothing better to do she dries the dishes after washing up. She sets the table for the morning. Five spoons and forks. Three knives. Five plates.

The Kidnappers

Her father had given her a new coloring book. He would only be in his lawyer's office a few minutes, he said. Ellie wanted to wait in the car and so he showed her how to push the button to lock it, how to pull the button up when he wanted back in. Not to open the door for anyone. He insisted they practice once. Then he stood looking at her for a moment through the window before he waved and jogged across the street.

It was a Wonder Woman coloring book. Ellie flipped through it, then turned back to the first page and started on the red and blue outfit Wonder Woman always wore. She was finishing the top that looked more like a bathing suit when a rapping on the window made her go way over the line. A woman in a green scarf and big sunglasses was calling her name, "Ellie, let me in."

"Mom," Ellie cried before pulling up the button. They both were crying as Ellie's mother pulled her from the car and together they ran down the sidewalk toward a red station wagon, Jane's car, her mother's writer-friend. Ellie scrambled across the front seat under the wheel and her mother followed and slammed the door. She pulled off the scarf and threw it into the back seat.

"God, Ellie." Their wet faces touched, then she started the car and pulled away, wheels scraping the sidewalk edge.

"We are going home," her mother said, her voice trembled, "home." She drove with one hand, holding Ellie's with the other. Maps crunched under Ellie's feet.

"Right now?" Ellie said. To her room, her toys, her friends.

"Right, now. We're on our way." Her mother snapped her sun-glasses off and put them on the seat. The buildings grew shorter beside piles of garbage as they drove faster than usual away from town, into the long curving miles of the highway that led to the inter-state that led toward home.

Ellie had missed her mother. Had missed cuddling her at night, their tee shirts touching, her mother's soft body curved around her for a short story about when she was a little girl before sleep sepa-rated them. Ellie had missed her sitting hunched over her typewriter looking into her head for a word. Sometimes Ellie held her breath until the typewriter began to beat again. Ellie had secretly hated the typewriter and sometimes pounded the top when she was alone with it. Until she had been given a smaller desk next to her mother's with a painted wooden sign that said "Sssssssssssh." Ten *s*'s. Was it still there?

Soon the car slowed and her mother stopped watching the rear-view mirror. She began telling Ellie about the new family on the block who had a little girl, eight years old just like Ellie. Telling Ellie about her new book. "I'm not just typing," her mother said once when she read Ellie's five-sentence essay about her parents. "My mother tipes," the essay said.

"It's what I type that matters," her mother said.

"You type what you write," Ellie said.

"And you print what you write," her mother said.

"So what."

Ellie closed her eyes and leaned her head back against her mother's shoulder. What was her father doing now? Was he missing her, com-ing out of the lawyer's office to the empty car, and her and the color-ing book gone?

Ellie woke just as they were pulling into the driveway. It was night. A small light on the porch hurt her eyes. Somebody finally must have replaced the bulb. Ellie's mother wiped her damp cheek and gave her a long hug. Ellie squeezed her harder than she ever had before. Then her mother began dumping stuff on the seat. The "key-hunt" they called it. At least one a day.

Later as Ellie slept on the couch with her head in her mother's lap,

her mother and Mrs. Conway from next door talked. They thought
she was sleeping, Ellie knew.

"He didn't follow you?"

"No, anyway all I had to do was cross the state line back into Illinois. I have custody here. I keep forgetting that after the horror of
the last few months." She smoothed Ellie's hair as she talked. Her
ring pulled, but not enough to hurt. "I feel like hell. Like a criminal,"
her mother said. "But I couldn't afford to go through the courts.
'Too much time and money,' my attorney said. And missing her all
that time. 'You go get her, or I can get you someone,' he told me, 'but
it's better if the parent goes along. Doesn't scare the kid as much.' So
here we are back."

"Just get settled and it will seem like it never happened," Mrs.
Conway said.

"But I had to do it," her mother said. "And anyway, he did it first."

She means *he* took me *first,* Ellie thought.

That was true. She remembered the day her father had picked her
up for the weekend. It had been hot and he was wearing a green
short-sleeved shirt that stuck to him, no jacket. They had gone to the
same hotel with the slide into the swimming pool and the pinball machines. Getting him up Saturday morning was always slow. First, he
sat on the edge of the bed blowing smoke all over the room and rubbing his eyes. Asking, "What's it doing outside?" Then he showered
and shaved, farting a lot. She always used the bathroom before he
got up. Finally, filled with pancakes and eggs, they went to the pool.
He taught her how to turn somersaults — pushing off from the bottom at just the right time. Knowing when the time was right. Ellie's
mother was afraid of water — learned to swim to graduate from college and forgot as soon as she passed. Ellie thought that was dumb.

Later they went to the zoo. The monkeys sat at the back of their
cages, hot and cranky, too tired to play. Ellie's father kept looking
for park benches. Ellie knew her father liked to sit a lot because
Ellie's mother used to yell at him about it. Now the television was
never on. Ellie missed it. The low buzz and glow from the family
room. It had taken her a while to get used to the silence after school.
Her mother always called, "Ellie?" which helped. After the zoo, on
the way back to the hotel, her father said he wanted her to live with

him for a while. Started off just like that. His eyes hadn't moved from the street. He missed her terribly, he said, and it wasn't fair that he was being deprived of her just because he was a man. "You're going to live with me for a while," he said, "just like you lived with your mother." Live where, Ellie thought, he usually just appeared in the car at the front of the house. She remembered crying because she was going to Molly's birthday party the next day. Her father never kept Kleenex in the car like her mother did. Ellie wiped her nose with her hand and then wiped her hand on the seat. He didn't see.

"You'll be able to see your mother," he said. "Just as soon as the courts work things out."

"But my new dress for Molly's party. Mom just finished it. Can't we go back for my dress?" It was home on her bed all laid out for tomorrow, its plaid sash hanging down to the floor.

"We'll buy you all new clothes," he said. Ellie didn't think he had any idea of all the millions of things girls wear.

"I want to go home," she said. Her hands were sticky from cotton candy and she had to go to the bathroom.

"I know, I know, but 'home' is going to be with me for a while."

They drove through the night. Once stopping by the side of the road where Ellie squatted down. Again no Kleenex. Once stopping for hamburgers and malts. Ellie ordered a big chocolate sundae that she couldn't finish. She hadn't looked at her father when she ordered it. The next day they bought shorts and halters that matched. And a canopy bed with a pink ruffle around the top that swayed in the breeze from her window. A jungle gym arrived two days later. Her father swore a lot when he worked, Ellie remembered. The neighborhood kids came around and watched. About laundry, "you're on your own," he told her. She learned to rummage in the still-dirty clothes for socks when she forgot to run the washer. Her father took her to his barber to have her hair 'styled.' "It's too short," she said, "that's what it *is*."

Her mother called. Finally she and Ellie talked while her father listened in. "I'll see you soon," her mother said. Ellie could hardly speak past her crying and then her father came in and hung up the phone. They ate hot dogs with ketchup, onions, mustard, relish. Hamburgers and TV dinners. His first girl friend was "Barbara," the second "Jude," but he called them all "love" so when the third one came to visit, Ellie didn't bother to learn her name.

And now fall was here and she was back with her mother. Everything looked strange and new for the first five minutes. The softness of the curtains and tablecloths and pillows was comforting. Her desk was still in place. It had a new sign, "Let's talk." Ellie liked the "Sssssssssh" better. She'd see Molly tomorrow, wear the new dress. She wondered if her father was angry. He would know she had opened the door because the window wasn't broken or anything. But she'd had to do it. She missed him too.

Two days later a man came to change the locks on the front and back doors. Her mother's friends touched her lightly as if she weren't quite real. They all heard the story of the trip back home. Angry voices puffed smoke. "The bastard," Ellie heard before her mother told her to go watch TV for a while. Her mother's friends were a bore, all that talk.

Ellie's mother walked her and Molly to school. Holding hands with them, skipping part way. Ellie wore her new skirt. They looked for Mrs. Logan's room. Mrs. Logan squeezed her and later chose her to write the date and quotation on the blackboard. It had taken her a while to print: *September 10, 1982 "Nothing in life is to be feared. It is to be understood." Marie Curie.* She stood aside while Mrs. Logan explained it and told a story about Marie Curie. Ellie turned back and forth so her skirt swished against her legs. Molly wanted one like it, she could tell.

Ellie knew her mother had talked with the principal. Miss Woodson was to call the police if anyone came for Ellie. Even her father. It had to stop.

Ellie liked walking back and forth to school with her mother. Once her mother said, "I think it's OK now, Ellie," but Ellie had insisted she put her shoes on and go along. "You have to," she said, making the hole in the screen door larger.

Ellie's hair was "growing in," her mother said. She still hunted for words — more often now, and for money. Looking out past her typewriter. Sometimes Ellie had a babysitter and her mother had dates.

They wore suits that looked alike and always asked Ellie the same questions. She did it back. "How many kids do you have? Where are they?" Some did, some didn't. Only one came now and stayed over sometimes. He wore jeans and a plaid shirt, sometimes no shoes. His toothbrush was red and hung next to her mother's. Ellie used it to scrub her nails. She always put it back. Sometimes he played Monopoly with her on Sunday while he watched football and her mother was cooking things that took too much time and didn't taste worth it. She'd slam the dice in front of him to get his attention. He'd jump but he never said anything. His name was Jack something.

She missed her father sometimes. She was allowed to talk to him now. He told her he would see her soon. It was complicated, he said. She hoped nobody like Barbara or Jude was sleeping in her canopy bed.

Field trips weren't really much fun. Just got teachers out of teaching. The bus ride was always too long, and the driver made them stop singing at the twentieth verse of "Another Bottle of Beer on the Wall." Allison, whose name was near Ellie's in the alphabet, usually spit up so that was an extra stop — if they made it in time.

The trip to the museum wasn't any different. Allison barfed two seats away. Ellie giggled and held her nose high in the air. Windows crashed open. The driver would clean it up while they were gone. They were each given a pamphlet for a game called "I spy." You had to look at a detail, like a dog's face, and then find it in a painting. Afterwards, Mrs. Logan lined them up by twos like babies and went to find the bus. Ellie and Molly held hands. A fight began in the back of the line and Ellie stepped out to look just as a pretty woman with red bushy hair came over and said, "Ellie?"

Ellie said, "Yes," and it seemed to be enough because suddenly behind the woman was a tall man who bent down and scooped Ellie up. Her chest collapsed and he pulled her against him. She tried to scream but no air came. "Ellie," Molly's cry followed her and she kicked her legs out but he was holding her too tight. Something was tearing open, cold air on her shoulder. He carried her down the steps two at a time, past the stone lions, carried her fast, making it difficult for the red-haired woman to keep up, telling Ellie that her father was waiting for her at the corner in the blue car over there and he wanted to see her very badly. The man's eyes were steamy red and he was panting like a dog into Ellie's face. "Put me down," she arched her back but it didn't work. "Hey, little girl," the man said, "in one minute now, OK."

"No," Ellie knew that somehow her father didn't want to just *see* her, like she wanted to just *see* him. And then they were in front of a car and her father was opening the door to the back seat. The man bent over and pushed her in. Her father held out his arms and they did feel good and big and he said, "Ellie, Ellie, Ellie," and then something about "your first ride in a little airplane, just like you always wanted." What did he know? The woman called, "Good-bye, Ellie"; she seemed about to say something more but turned away. The woman's voice, not like her mother's at all, made her cry harder. No Kleenex, just her father's rough suit, but she didn't care.

The airport was too small. They drove right up to the toy plane and the pilot led them up the steep steps, saying as soon as they got off the ground he would let her fly the plane. Had she ever flown a plane before? His teeth glistened. The dumb shit, Ellie thought. She could hear her father say just that.

But he told her he had a new sales job and that's where they were going. Her canopy bed was already there with a new pink quilt. All girls like pink.

"It sucks," Ellie said. "Sucks" was new at school, it was the first time Ellie used it. It didn't make her feel better.

"Forget that talk." Her father patted her knee.

"Where we going?" she asked, but he couldn't tell her right now. A new place.

"Will we be there long?" she asked.

"We're going to live there. You know—cook and sleep there."

"And watch TV."

"Quit talking like your mother."

"I like TV," Ellie said, her eyes filling again. "How long are we going to live there? When will I see Mom?"

"Oh, Ellie, Ellie." He put his arm around her. "Not right away. I'm sorry it has to be that way—but the same thing would happen just like before. It has to end sometime."

The plane made Ellie sick, lurching into slides she felt inside her stomach. She didn't want to fly. Would she barf like Allison, make the pilot mad? She felt wet all over. Her father talked on about the new school, the teacher expecting her. Ellie wondered if the teacher knew she had a mother.

The teacher called her "Ellen." "Ellen, stop daydreaming," and Ellie tried. This school was smaller, just like her father said. The whole town seemed a smaller version of where she lived with her mother, except people were outside their houses more, planting things, chopping wood, waxing cars, cutting hair. She missed her mother, and this missing brought an ache that made it hard to eat. She hadn't seen or talked with her since the museum. She was sure her mother was still alive. Only grandmothers die. Her father said of course she'd see her mother again. But she didn't think she would see her mother here. Strange how the words "daddy" and "mom" had become "your father" and "your mother." They seemed to accuse her of something. "Your mother" was far away, she knew. At least three plane-hours away. When she thought about her mother she sometimes held her breath. She didn't know what to do.

She began to forget what clothes she had. Her father never separated the dirty laundry into piles and so her blouses grew gray and limp. One turned pink — at least she couldn't remember *buying* a pink blouse. She learned to throw a baseball. They took bike rides along roads with trucks that seemed to pull at her hair as they passed. She ate breakfast alone trying to forget her dreams, but her throat was always sore. She woke screaming one night when she fell down three steps to the landing in the middle of the stairs. At home, at her mother's house, the bathroom was *that way* down the hall. She lay there until she realized where she was. Until her father told her, lifting her, "You must have been sleepwalking," as he tucked her into bed. Ellie felt such tightness in her chest that she couldn't feel the bed under her. Or the blanket above. Her teacher asked about the bruise and her explanation sounded silly.

She knew now where she lived because it was on signs in town. The grocery store was called "Granada's Largest Market for Fit Produce." Where do they sell maps, she wondered. Wyoming?

Her father had more loves who probably had names. They smelled good and sometimes brought overnight bags with fun compartments. The latest cooked special breakfasts of very very mushy eggs and crisp bacon. She put green things in the eggs and turned their orange juice pink with something from her father's liquor cabinet. She played cards with Ellie and fixed her hair as they all sat in front of the TV glow.

Ellie's father became president of the P.T.A. "Men are usually just treasurers," her teacher said, "You should be proud."

After three months Ellie was allowed to walk home alone from school. Oh, not really alone, because her friend Juanita joined up with her after the fourth block going and up to the fourth block coming home. Home? One of them, anyway.

The car was on its third time around the block. She hadn't noticed it the first two times until the third and then she realized all three. Did that make sense?

The car was going slower. She looked over at the driver. He was a man she didn't know. But she didn't know everyone in town yet. She put her lunch box down by a lamp post, and then she kept on walking.

The car, it was green, not too new, speeded up to be a little ahead of her, then stopped. She kept on walking.

"Hello, little girl," he said. He raised his eyebrows, instead of smiling, she thought.

She was surprised he didn't know her name. She stopped.

"You don't know my name?"

"Uh, no," he said. His hair was shorter than her father's hair. It looked molded to his head like puppet's hair. "Do you want me to guess your name?" He asked softly as if there were someone else around to hear.

"No," Ellie said.

"You know," he said. "I just saw an ice-cream store back a couple blocks and I bet you like ice cream." He didn't seem to be asking her anything so she didn't reply. She looked back at her lunch box sitting by the lamp post.

"Why don't you come with me and we'll go get an ice-cream cone. I'll let you have double scoops."

"You don't know my father, do you," she said.

He hesitated and adjusted his mirror.

"Or my mother," she said. "Do you know them?"

"No," he said shaking his head, "I don't believe I've met them."

A car came by and he watched it pass without speaking.

Ellie watched him. He turned back to her, his eyebrows pulling up a smile this time.

"Can I have a triple scoop?" she asked. Did her father mind her having ice cream before dinner? She couldn't remember for sure. Maybe it was her mother?

"Sure," he said. "Sure."

She walked around the front of the car and opened the door herself. Then she got in and closed the door. Herself. The radio was playing something fast and loud. He must have turned it on while she was walking around the car. She sat back as the car pulled away from the curb. She folded her hands in her lap.

"I thought we'd take a ride first," he said. He lit a cigarette. It smelled sweet.

Ellie closed her eyes and breathed deep. She felt the car speed up on its ride away from town. She wanted to go back but she didn't know where. Now, as her mom and dad both said, it simply had to end.

Getting to Know the Weather

She has been watching them for two weeks: women named Lou and Betty and Alice. Gert, Ellie, or Kay, or Irene — their names on plastic tags, in white stitching on a pocket or on gold pins holding a lacy handkerchief in place. She chooses a good seat at a different lunch counter each day. Droops her coat around her lap, the sleeves pulled across her stomach, and orders coffee, sometimes scrambled eggs or an English muffin when she can't resist the smell of melting butter as it foams. But her money is running out and even though she feels her training isn't quite complete, today is the day.

She sits and watches the women work. Her wrists feel the motions they make spreading chicken salad on a slice of toast, cutting Danish for the grill, or shaking a can of whipped cream. Each woman has distinctive flourishes — an extra swipe with the knife, or a small flip that pings the silverware when it is set down. But Jessie knows it is people watching, even her own watching, that makes these women put together such dramatic stage gestures — customers are more appreciative than any husband or kids. She needs to remember that deftness matters, to practice with peanut butter tonight. Jessie, at forty-five, knows without question that the men who manage lunch counters in these small midwestern towns can tell who's worked as a waitress before. She needs a job her first try — it will be her first real job, not counting the chickens she used to keep for eggs, or the peach preserves or corn relish she put up to sell at the church fairs for twenty years in Irwin.

This town has three possibilities; Kresge's where she now sits under a too-garish light, but she could get used to it. They have good hamburgers and the nicest cosmetic counter of things she wants to try—cream rouge, eyeliner, body powders called Evening in Paris and Wind Song. Then there is Woolworth's just like the one back home in Pennsylvania with oiled dark floors and bolts of cloth too near the front doors. But their counters are bright red and clean and the waitresses wear little green aprons, starched and welcoming to tips. Today Woolworth's put a sign in the window: COUNTER HELP WANTED. After her coffee she'll go over and apply. Finally there is the coffee counter at the bus station, but it is last choice. She went back twice after coming into town on the cross-country run from Pittsburgh. Too much noise from the jukebox and traveling radios against a lingering level of bus exhaust worse than a cloud of burned onions. The people come and go from too many places to ever see a familiar face again—some you wouldn't want to. She wants to know her customers—even the mean ones who only leave a quarter rather than dig deeper for an extra nickel or dime.

Marge is on the morning shift as Jessie slides into her seat beside the cash register. She's been practicing on Marge. Marge has the flair she wants. Marge's apricot hair is fluffed under a wispy net. Jessie has one in her pocket just like it. Marge's cheeks glitter more than usual—tiny specks of silver or gold floating on soft red ponds. Jessie never wears rouge and this has been hard to get used to. Now each night in her housekeeping room she applies it liberally to the "apples of her smile," as the counter girl put it. Her husband and kids wouldn't recognize her just because of the new color in her cheeks. But all waitresses wear it—Jessie can tell it is more important than lipstick although some waitresses keep a tube in their pockets and use the side of the coffee machine or toaster to reapply it just before their men customers come in.

"Morning. Coffee?" Marge pulls a white paper napkin out of the holder and swoops it down an instant before the spoon lands on it dead center, without a sound.

Jessie nods first, then says, "Hi, Marge. Coffee. Maybe a muffin today if you have any." She forces herself to say Marge's name even though she doesn't really know her.

Marge writes 'cf' and 'mf' on her tiny green pad, not keeping to the lines. The pencil is dull and leaves a trail of wide lead as 'mf' drifts off the page. Pad into her pocket and pencil into her hair. Jessie will have to let her hair grow.

"Still raining out there?" Marge asks, pouring a high dark steaming arc of coffee into a white mug.

"Rain?" Jessie never knows what the weather is. Showers or record heat waves always surprise her. Is it still raining? She's been looking at powder puffs and nail polish for the last five minutes. It is a question she'll have to learn to ask, sighing heavily over lingering storms, rolling her eyes at three inches of snow and her stuck at work without any boots, and the buses probably running late, or her ride not showing up. Or fanning herself with a plastic menu against the July heat or the air conditioning on the blink again.

Marge brings her muffin and pulls up a knife, a butter pat, and a tiny plastic container of jelly from under the counter. Jessie likes this miniature world.

"Muffins just come in," Marge says, giving the small round plate an extra twist in front of Jessie. "More coffee yet?" Jessie notes the "yet." It makes her feel cared for.

Like Mr. Arnold must feel. Once or twice a day he comes in from First National Bank. The shoulders of his coat are dark and he runs a hand over his thin wet hair.

"Morning, Mr. Arnold, still raining I can see." Marge pours him a black coffee and tempts him with the pastry tray. "Ten days straight. It don't quit we're going to have to dry out our money." Jessie marvels that Marge has actually counted days.

"Make it a grilled Danish today, Marge. I need something to lift my spirits," he says. But Jessie knows Marge already did that.

Next Mrs. Penrose, a plump cashier from the grocery store, comes in for six coffees to go. As Marge fits their lids on tight, the woman hands across a picture of her new grandson. He is the most beautiful baby Marge has ever seen. She holds the picture carefully by the edges and steps down the counter to include Jessie and Mr. Arnold in the viewing of a scrawny yellow wrinkled face. "Look at that face," Marge says. She is serious.

The clock, red with fruity numbers, probably from Kresge's own kitchen department, says 10:30. Few customers come in so Jessie lingers. Marge works around her as if Jessie is an anchor. She wipes the surfaces of the counters, checks to see the salt lids are on tight, and marries the ketchup bottles, placing one on top of the other. The record department is playing "Raindrops Keep Falling on My Head," which makes Marge inexplicably roll her eyes. As Marge works she tells Jessie all about her daughter who just had twins and already gave one of them a haircut. "Shaved his head is what it amounts to. Just so she could tell them apart."

Jessie sips her coffee sympathetically. She tells Marge teeth will do it. Marge should pass that along to her daughter. "No two people have identical teeth — like fingerprints — I know from my own son's twins," Jessie says.

Marge stops wiping. Her cloth, stationary, smells sour. "Imagine that. We both got twins in the family. It's a small world."

Jessie has imagined it. Her two kids are off working and not even thinking about having families. She'd like twins. But it might have been hard to leave grandchildren behind. "One's lost three baby teeth and the other five. Teeth do it."

Marge looks relieved. Jessie has come to realize that just saying things brightens someone's day. She always suspected this. Her own parents and sisters talked and talked. But George never got over their having to get married. "Just a little earlier than planned," she said to him, trying not to cry, back when they were both graduating from high school in a record class of seventeen. Today kids have it nice. Pills and women's magazines talking about real things instead of meat loaf recipes or thirty ways to make your husband happy. But George didn't have a reply and after they married he settled into an early silence that spread a pall on the kids even before they could talk. It sent her friends from the Fire Hall Ladies Aid away too. And now her question to herself is not what she ever saw in him, but what she ever heard from him.

Jessie planned her exit a long time. When the kids were in high school she walked the mile and a half into town past the neighbors' farms that were farms in name only, the chickens and cows long since sold off, the tractors dead in the overgrown fields, men in the mills making steel. In those days she sat at the lunch counters to watch the counter girls cutting pies, cleaning coffee urns as big as the old milker in the barn. She admired their self-assurance, the perky hats they wore, their pockets gray and heavy with tips. The way they slid coins off the counter into their hands like men palming poker winnings. Talking back to sly managers, calling orders to sassy cooks. Ringing the register and catching the drawer with cushioned stomachs. She looked for wedding rings, signs of marriage or kids. Most were single with birthstones on their right hands, women who a generation ago would have been the resident spinster aunts. She imagined apartments or rooms where they put their feet up and complained about the hours, the sass, the tips, to the woman upstairs who heard them come in and wandered down to talk. She expected to find she was over the hill but her first visit reassured her that women her age, extra pounds around their middle, hadn't been pushed aside by the shrill teenagers who worked at the drive-in places and Dairy Queens. A few high school girls came to work the late Thursday and Saturday shifts but their hearts weren't on the weather or keeping the counters clean. Their friends lounged around learning to smoke, sneaking doughnuts, applying coats of fuchsia nail polish, waiting for closing time. But Jessie didn't want a job in Irwin anyway — too close to home.

Instead she saved money for a red collapsible suitcase which she kept folded in her pantry till she could also afford a one-way bus ticket to somewhere in Indiana and a place to stay for a month. She planned to go to a large city, say Indianapolis, and work her way out of town till she came to a place that suited her. She'd know it when she saw it. She chose Indiana because no one talked about it except for the top part cut through by I-90 on the way to Chicago.

When her youngest, her daughter, was a senior, she began to make lists of things she would take along. Long lists at first, her despair directly proportional to the size and number of items. Her heart lightened as she crossed things off. This was hard on her because she suspected George would begin selling her stuff as soon as he realized she was gone for good. When their children's departures seemed permanent George had carried Susie's canopy bed and Mike's aquarium out to the front lawn for a yard sale. Jessie can still see the pink eyelet canopy fluttering in the breeze, catching the eye of a passing motorist better than any sign could do. A month later the children sulkily enumerated to her the lost items of their childhood, carting off remaining records and scrapbooks that Jessie had hidden from the sale. "I'm going to close them rooms off and save heat," George said.

Jessie's final list included: her mother's amber necklace, her mother's ivory hand mirror, pictures of the kids, one dress, one skirt, two blouses, underwear, one nightgown, comb and brush, the 1937 *World Atlas*—sure she knew the world had changed, but Indiana hadn't—and the family Bible.

The last day, waiting to go for the one-o'clock bus, Jessie packed in the pantry. Then she wandered around the house touching things she regretted leaving: her mother's cherry sideboard, the rocking chair she'd used for nursing Mike and Susie, the braided rug she made for the front room, her teacup collection used but once for the Ladies Aid. She fretted about a note for George. What could she say that wouldn't run on into angry words? She simply couldn't think of a thing to say—considering it might be showed around. But she had to leave a sign—in all fairness he had to know.

Suddenly it came to her. She went down to his toolroom in the basement and returned with the tiny red circles he had used for the yard sale. Then she set about pricing the sideboard, rug, teacups, dining room table, and other stuff he'd consider hers—fair prices in black ink with a little room for bargaining. This was information enough; she figured he'd know what to do.

She was nervous buying her ticket and might not have found her voice except for a radio blaring from someone's shoulder. "Speak up," the ticket man yelled. Selling tickets didn't appeal to Jessie. She studied other people's jobs. Grocery stores didn't allow time to visit with customers as clerks shoved lettuce and meat on to the bag boy. Bank clerks were too prissy, and maybe you needed college to take care of all that money. Factory jobs she didn't know about. Anyway her mind was made up.

She got on the bus and settled into a seat to watch the landscapes go by the wide tinted window. This was her first trip in a direction other than north to Niagara Falls. When a sign welcomed her to Ohio she put her head back and said good-bye to Pennsylvania and George.

Jessie hopes her blouse isn't wrinkled. Last night she borrowed an iron from upstairs, from a retired couple who write letters to people whose books they read. They collect answers. Jessie takes out a new compact of rouge and lipstick and adds some color, glancing at Marge to see exactly where the red spots should be.

She leaves Marge 35¢ and says as she puts on her coat that maybe the rain is letting up.

Marge shrugs elaborately. "I'll keep your cup in place for a refill. Come back if it's too wet." Tears blur Jessie's eyes — it's all in what's said.

The rain has stopped. Jessie walks three blocks to Woolworth's, past a post office, a hardware store, a dress shop, and a bank and stops across the street. She wants this job. She can't remember wanting anything as bad ever before.

The help-wanted sign is still in the center window near the display of lunch boxes shaped like houses landscaped with pink tennis shoes.

The pungent smell of grilled and rolling hot dogs provides a special warmth from wet streets. They have the best hot dogs in town. Jessie straightens her shoulders, taking five years off her age according to *Women's Day*. Two people are sitting at the counter, a postman with his leather bag at his feet and a lady in a flat rain hat writing in her checkbook with a red pen. "Helen" is slicing a blueberry pie while the postman watches, tapping his foot. Jessie knows he will have a piece, maybe two.

Helen points her toward the manager's office, a tiny black room partitioned off from a display of wall lamps and frilly curtains. "Rain finally stopped?" Helen calls after her.

"For at least ten minutes," Jessie says, happy to have a sentence to propel her to the back of the store.

Mr. Martin looks up from his littered desk as she knocks on the door frame. Everything about him seems concave, his chest, his cheeks, his wide forehead.

She tells him she is looking for a job. He motions to a chair. "Any experience?" he asks. "I gotta have girls who already know what they're doing."

"I've been a waitress for the past fifteen years in Irwin, that's in Pennsylvania." The twins come to mind. "At a Woolworth's there, a counter almost identical to your set-up." She cranes her neck to bring Helen and the pies into view as if to make absolutely certain of her comparisons. "Training new help can really be a pain," Jessie says, trying to make her eyes reflect broken dishes and lost revenues from people she has worked with in her fifteen years. At Woolworth's.

"Good. Then you probably still got a Woolworth's employee number on file." He picks up a pencil.

"Oh, that," Jessie says. "For the past two years I've been at Sun Drugs."

Mr. Martin says, "Oh." His gaze wanders back to his desk to diagrams of windows and screens. "That number would be nice. Saves paperwork. Don't suppose you have any old uniforms?"

"Lost too much weight," Jessie says. "A move does that to you. I moved out here to be near my married daughter."

"She got any kids? You wouldn't be taking time off for babysitting, nothing like that."

No twins. "No kids. She don't want any." Jessie shrugs elaborately —like Marge. "Times have changed."

He agrees with her, heartily tapping his approval with his pencil. She admires his lunch box window, the bright lights of the counter. He tells her the hours, where she can get uniforms. When to come in. "Helen'll show you the ropes tomorrow morning, you can double on her shift the first two days." He swings around in his chair. "Still raining?"

Jessie rises. "Stopped, but not for long," she says, "looks like it'll keep up through the week." He is cheered by this as if she predicted tropical temperatures. He laughs and she laughs too.

"Tell Helen to take the sign out of the window," he says.

Helen gives her a cup of coffee and says to come in at nine. She has been working here ten years. "Nine," the mailman corrects, naming the year of the fire next door. Hand on her ample hip, Helen says some people just notice too much but her posture improves as she says it. The mailman heaves his bag up as if it were weightless and waves.

Jessie buys two uniforms and two aprons, both a trifle snug because she is going to lose weight. She buys a blue ceramic pitcher which she'll use later for flowers. That evening she tries the uniforms on, standing in front of her dresser mirror, her hair net floating in place. She has to be convincing when Mr. Martin comes by for coffee. She practices her pour. Her arm lifts the blue pitcher at the same instant the water begins to pour forward into the sink.

The calendar hanging on the back of the door tells her she has been away twelve going on thirteen days. The calendar has fuzzy pictures of flowers whose names she doesn't know. Flowers that look like they grow indoors in small spaces. They give the room color—like her rouge. She isn't going to do any more in the way of furnishings for now. She likes not having one thing that needs to be picked up and dusted. She likes the silent TV in the corner of the room, its face to the wall. She has the bed to herself. Lord is she tired. Not too tired for a hot bath and maybe a short visit with the couple upstairs. Letter to her daughter later. It's a job, she'll say. Hard on the feet, but it's a job.

ILLINOIS SHORT FICTION

Crossings by Stephen Minot
A Season for Unnatural Causes by Philip F. O'Connor
Curving Road by John Stewart
Such Waltzing Was Not Easy by Gordon Weaver

Rolling All the Time by James Ballard
Love in the Winter by Daniel Curley
To Byzantium by Andrew Fetler
Small Moments by Nancy Huddleston Packer

One More River by Lester Goldberg
The Tennis Player by Kent Nelson
A Horse of Another Color by Carolyn Osborn
The Pleasures of Manhood by Robley Wilson, Jr.

The New World by Russell Banks
The Actes and Monuments by John William Corrington
Virginia Reels by William Hoffman
Up Where I Used to Live by Max Schott

The Return of Service by Jonathan Baumbach
On the Edge of the Desert by Gladys Swan
Surviving Adverse Seasons by Barry Targan
The Gasoline Wars by Jean Thompson

Desirable Aliens by John Bovey
Naming Things by H. E. Francis
Transports and Disgraces by Robert Henson
The Calling by Mary Gray Hughes